THE
TRUE
COLOURS
OF
CORAL
GLEN

JULIETTE FORREST

MSCHOLASTIC

FOR MUM. DAD
AND ROBERT

Scholastic Children's Books
An imprint of Scholastic Ltd
Euston House, 24 Eversholt Street, London, NW1 1DB, UK
Registered office: Westfield Road, Southam, Warwickshire, CV47 0RA
SCHOLASTIC and associated logos are trademarks and/or
registered trademarks of Scholastic Inc.

First published in the UK by Scholastic Ltd, 2019

Text copyright © Juliette Forrest, 2019
Cover illustration by Jamie Gregory

The right of Juliette Forrest to be identified
as the author of this work has been asserted.

ISBN 978 1407 19322 9

A CIP catalogue record for this book
is available from the British Library.

Printed by CPI Group (UK) Ltd, Croydon, CR0 4YY
Papers used by Scholastic Children's Books are made
from wood grown in sustainable forests.

a... ... ... idents
... are used
... dead,

CHAPTER

1

Every night, when the moon showed up and the *Tinfoil* clouds parted like curtains to reveal the stars, I slept in a rainbow. You wouldn't find any flowery wallpaper, world maps or posters of fluffy kittens in my room: it was floor-to-ceiling covered in paint charts. Small, every-colour-under-the-sun rectangles were the first thing I glimpsed in the morning and the last thing I saw in the evening.

Mum said my walls were so busy she was amazed I didn't suffer from double vision. And Dad would get distracted by all the different shades and sometimes forget what he'd come into my room to tell me. Gran always pointed to the same tiny patch of silver, next to the wardrobe, and said *Stardust Highway* was her favourite name of a colour *ever*. I loved what the paints were called because yellow was never plain old boring yellow: it was *Sunshiny Days* or *Tropical Smoothie* or *Downy Duckling* or *Luscious Lemon Drops* or *Treasure Island Gold*. When I'd get home from school, Gran would ask me how my day had been and I'd always answer her with a colour. If I'd had double art, I'd say something along the lines of *Sunbeam Glow*, but if I'd sat a maths test, I would mutter *Stormy Canyon*. And if I just wanted to make Gran snort, I'd tell her *Sailor's Kiss*.

But we won't be able to do this any more.

Gran died on Saturday and there isn't a colour on the planet that could sum up how heartbroken I am, because it was my fault.

CHAPTER 2

God was missing. He was *Midnight Oasis Black* and lopsided because of all the fights he'd been in. Gran had taken him in off the streets and swore he was part ragamuffin and part panther. She took us in off the streets too after Dad lost his job. And even though he got a new one ages ago, we never left. Dad told me Gran loved having us there because the house had felt big and empty since Grandpa died. He went to heaven when I was a baby, but I announced to everyone at the breakfast table that I'd seen Grandpa, once, standing in the hallway,

3

and I knew it was him from their wedding photo on the mantelpiece. Grandpa glowed *Celestial Spark* and had smiled at me, but I stopped going to the bathroom in the middle of the night, just in case he appeared again.

A whoosh of air had escaped from Dad's mouth and he'd ruffled my hair. He said I had an *overactive imagination* and I'd grinned because it made me sound really clever. Mum spilled her tea and Gran had given me a hug a bear would be jealous of.

Before God disappeared, if he wasn't roaming the streets, he'd be stretched out on Gran's lap. His purr sounded more like a rattle, as if something inside him had come loose and knocked against his ribcage. Gran had named him Godfrey after the lead actor in the film *The Blood on Satan's Claw*. I think that was because, until we put the bell on God's collar, he'd leave us a gift of a small dead furry creature on the back doorstep, every night.

I checked the chestnut tree in the garden for God first, because he loved sitting in high up places too. Under the broad *Chic Lime* leaves, I could only spot a pigeon preening itself. When the rest of the kids in art drew pigeons, they always coloured them in *Elephant Breath*, as though they couldn't see the shiny *Amethyst Reflections* or *Green Genie* in their feathers or their *Orange Squash* feet. The pigeon flapped its wings and I didn't hang about because it's not wise to stand underneath one for long. Grown-ups believe it's good luck to get hit by bird poop, except I think they just say that to make themselves feel better because they were unfortunate enough to get splatted in the first place.

Sticking my head into all the shrubs, I scoured the flower beds for signs of God's footprints. I knew exactly what to look for because if Gran ever made a trifle and forgot to put it in the fridge, he'd walk over the top of it, leaving paw marks in the cream.

I even went into the shed, which was full of stuff nobody wanted but couldn't bring themselves to throw away. Once I'd managed to squeeze myself inside, I called God's name and stood still in the hope I'd detect a scratch or a yowl or a hiss. All I could hear was my breathing and seagulls on the chimney tops making the same noises as rusty swings.

I spied a box in the corner. It wasn't unknown for God to snooze in places you would think were impossible to fall asleep in; I'd once found him in the oven, which fortunately hadn't been switched on.

Easing my way through a narrow gap between a dusty table and a leaning lampstand, I peered into the gloom, but God was nowhere to be seen. The box was stuffed with candleholders, old packs of cards, cutlery, a vase and a photo in a cracked glass frame. The picture was of me on holiday at Loch Tay, standing with my belly out, wearing my old swimming costume with *Bashful Pink* flamingos on it. I had my goggles on over my curly *Golden Spice* hair and was squinting at the camera. I remembered how the wood had been warm and rough under my bare feet, and the air had smelled of hot skin, suntan lotion and sweet water.

"You didn't smile, Coral! You gurned!" Gran had said after she'd taken the photo.

I'd been too busy peering at a thick tangle of seaweed, wondering what could be lurking in amongst it, to answer her. I'd once watched a wildlife documentary on great white sharks. They have three hundred teeth in seven rows and can smell their prey from over two miles away. After discovering this, I'd walked around the puddles in the park for weeks afterwards. And if a duck disappeared from the surface of the pond, I'd made Gran stay until it had safely bobbed back up again.

"Your dad used to love this place when he was your age. Your grandfather and I were convinced he was half boy and half seal because he was never out of the water." Gran's eyes had sparkled mischievously; they shone brighter than the summer sun playing on the loch. "Mind you," she added, "some people are of the opinion boys are braver than girls."

I had glared at her through my goggles. "Girls can be just as brave as boys, if not even braver." I'd filled my lungs, pinched my nose and leapt forward into the unknown.

The iciness of the loch had taken my breath away. Every part of me went numb, except for my heart, which had thumped painfully with the shock of it all.

That was exactly how I'd felt when Mum and Dad broke the news Gran had died.

The cry of the seagulls brought me back to the shed.

This is all your fault. All. Your. Fault.

My thoughts made me tremble and everything spun. My fingers left marks in the dust on the tabletop.

Searching for God took my mind off what I had done for a while, but something inside me weighed me down heavier than anchors.

What I would give to have one more minute with Gran.

I sniffed loudly and wiped my eyes. I locked the shed and strode towards the house, the gravel crunching under my feet. A robin landed on the wall, tilting its head at me before flapping off into Miss Mirk's garden.

Hoisting myself on to the wall, I was careful not to scrape my knees or sit on dried bird poop. I peered up at Miss Mirk's windows. The blinds were always down and there was a tear in one of them near the bottom that I was convinced she used as a spyhole. Miss Mirk was our neighbour and to be avoided at all cost. When she wheeled her shopping trolley

8

along the street, she walked more like Dad than Mum. And she spoke so quietly you had to lean in way closer than you wanted to, to catch what she was saying, which was usually a complaint.

I'd climbed this wall ever since my parents had warned me not to, and I knew every inch of Miss Mirk's garden. The place was overgrown: killer weeds and rosette-winning dandelions burst out from between the patio slabs. Branches hung down, covering the shed, that looked as though it had been dropped into her garden from a great height. Gran always said she wouldn't have been at all surprised if there was a velociraptor lurking in the bushes.

Glancing at her house, I caught a movement behind the hole in the blind.

I swung my leg over the wall and lowered myself to the ground. There was no way God would be visiting with Miss Mirk; he was far too fussy about the company he kept.

God had meant everything to Gran and that was why I was going to find him. For the past five nights, I'd left out turkey-flavoured cat food. I don't even know why God loved it so much. I suppose

9

if you eat mice, turkey probably tastes a whole lot better. Tempting or not, the food was always there, untouched, in the morning. Dad said I shouldn't worry as God would also be upset over Gran and he'd come home as soon as he was good and ready.

Running away had crossed my mind. I couldn't even gaze out of the window without thinking I'd catch sight of Gran potting plants in the greenhouse and every time I wandered into the kitchen, I expected to find her there, smiling. When I realized the room was empty, it struck me that she really had gone and it was as if an invisible boxing glove had just punched me in the stomach.

The truth was, it wouldn't matter if I was here or a trillion miles away; I would still feel wretched. I couldn't leave; I had to find God, and besides, Gran's funeral was tomorrow.

Thinking about it made my insides twist and knot like a balloon animal.

"Hey, Coral," said Dad, as he dripped some sauce from a packet into a pan. It hissed and bubbled as he stirred it vigorously. "Any luck?"

"Nope," I said, glancing at Gran's empty chair.

Dad jiggled the pan over the gas ring, sending slivers of carrot flying on to the cooker. He swore under his breath – something he only ever usually did in the car. If Gran had been here, she'd have bumped Dad out of the way with her hip and grabbed the wooden spoon. Then she'd have told me what she'd been up to that afternoon. She always had something going on, like her, Nessie, Dodo and Margot picketing the golf club for not allowing ladies in, or protesting outside Marlena Hatchette's boutique because it sold coats and gloves with real fur on them. Once they'd even made the news by chaining themselves to an ancient oak tree the council eventually sawed down. Sometimes Gran would get sad and say being old and wise didn't count for much these days. Then she'd brighten her voice and tell me I couldn't possibly solve all of the world's problems, but I could make a difference by choosing one thing I believed in to fight tooth and nail for.

The front door slammed, snapping me out of my thoughts.

"Sorry I'm late," said Mum, sweeping into the kitchen. She was carrying so many bags she resembled the donkey from Buckaroo!, the second before it threw everything off.

"I dropped in at the florist's on the way home." Mum plonked the shopping on the floor, shrinking in size when she kicked her heels off. A sigh escaped her perfectly glossy lips as she sat. Even though she worked at the Miracles™ cosmetics counter at the local department store, there were dark circles under her eyes. I guess she was having difficulty sleeping too.

"Dinner is served." Dad lifted the pan over to the dishes and hesitated, realizing he'd put out four plates instead of three. He shoved the extra one back into the cupboard. All of us were finding it hard that Gran had gone. I've heard people on DIY SOS say the kitchen was the heart of the home except, in our household, it was Gran.

Dad brought the plates over to the table, plonking them in front of us. He rifled through the cupboard for his chilli sauce. He preferred his food on the hot side and Gran always used to remark she was surprised his head was still attached to his shoulders.

"How are you?" Mum asked me.

"Can't find God anywhere." I carefully moved the mushrooms to the side of my plate.

"Don't do that," she scolded. "They are full of B vitamins – which keep us naturally beautiful without the use of chemically laden, overpriced skin creams. But the real secret of beauty is smiling, not that Miracles™ cosmetics want you to know this."

I rolled my eyes. As far as I was concerned there would never come a day it was OK to eat fungus, and smiling wasn't at the top of my list right now.

"Perhaps we should ask the neighbours to check their sheds or cellars? Cats are always getting shut away in places they shouldn't be." Dad returned to the table with the sauce.

I thought about the poster I'd seen every morning on the way to school. It had been taped to the lamp post at the bus stop and had a picture of a Jack Russell on it. The dog's name was Nip and there were big letters saying "REWARD" above its head. It had been there for weeks and the rain was making the terrier fade and "REWARD" smudge. I hoped Nip was found before he disappeared from the poster altogether.

"Can I make a missing poster, Dad? I could stick copies around the street and put them through neighbours' doors." I took a small mouthful of carrot.

"Good idea, Coral." Dad yanked the top off the chilli sauce.

"Could you give me a hand with it?" I laid down my fork.

"I'm sure we can fit it in at some point." Dad was a graphic designer. It was his job to make websites and brochures look cool and sometimes he designed posters as a hobby in his spare time. If he was happy, he'd do stuff so bright you could probably spot it from space, and if his football team lost a match, the posters would be in monochrome. It was Dad who named me Coral, after his favourite colour. Mum told me it meant *daughter of the sea* but Gran and I came across a book in the library that said: *coral will inspire you to conquer your fears and be bolder in your choices.* I'm not sure that was true because sometimes I still sleep with the light on.

"I could hand the posters in at the vet's and the newsagent's." Mum passed Dad the salt. "And there's a communal noticeboard at the supermarket."

"There's a local website for missing pets," added Dad. "John from work mentioned it when their rabbits vanished."

"Did they find them?" I speared some broccoli with my fork.

Dad paused. "Not yet. But they will, I'm sure."

They wanted God home as much as I did. And this made me feel a little bit less miserable inside, and then much worse.

God would still be with us if Gran was here. And Gran would still be here if you hadn't...

"I'm going to make a start on the poster." I scraped my chair back.

Mum and Dad glanced at each other. I could tell there was something they wanted to say but they weren't sure how to say it. After Dad finished chewing his mouthful, he cleared his throat. "We'd like a word with you."

My heart felt as if it was a horse galloping down a racetrack with hurdles.

They know what happened the day that Gran died.

"Would you rather stay at home tomorrow? Neither your dad or I would be upset if you didn't want to be at the funeral; it wouldn't mean you love Gran any less," said Mum.

"I'll go." My stomach flipped as I got to my feet awkwardly.

"Do you have anything you want to ask us about tomorrow?" Dad rubbed his beard, which had grown dark and scratchy. The events of the past few days had not just changed him on the inside; they'd made him different on the outside too.

I licked my lips. I wanted to ask if there would ever be a time when the pain of losing Gran didn't make my body ache from head to toe. And how I could live with myself after what I'd done. And if it was possible for a heart that was broken into a million pieces to mend itself.

But nothing came out.

"If at any point it gets too upsetting, one of us will bring you home. There is no right or wrong way to be at a funeral; everyone reacts differently.

Some people might be completely overwhelmed by their sadness. Others might joke and laugh at the reception afterwards, and that's OK too. Funerals are not just about mourning the loss of someone, they're also about celebrating a person's life – and your gran was a wonderful lady whom we love very much." Dad kept his voice steady, but his eyes reddened as they became shinier.

All the stuck words burned my throat. I swallowed hard and they tumbled into the pit of my stomach, where they sat heavy as bricks.

"We'll do the dishes tonight. I have something for you, so I'll pop up later," said Mum.

Before I went to my room, I slipped into the cloakroom. It was warm and dark. The gas meter clicked and whirred heartbeat-soft. I stood between the coats and scarves, breathing in. I could smell Gran's rose and geranium perfume in the air, almost as if she was still here.

CHAPTER
3

"You look lovely, Coral," said Dad, straightening his *Caviar Black* tie in the hall mirror. He smiled, except it wasn't a real one because I couldn't see his teeth.

Mum was the only one being honest with her feelings. Earlier this morning, she'd remembered Gran used to hide her wedding rings in the sugar bowl to keep them safe, and one year they'd ended up in the Christmas pudding, much to the surprise of Great-Aunt Winnie, who'd cracked her dentures on them. Mum's hand had covered her eyes and her laughter turned into sobs. I'd watched her shoulders

18

rise and fall as her breath had shuddered, and even though I'd just spread lemon curd on my toast, I'd put it in the bin and made Mum a cup of tea.

My dress was too tight and the backs of my new shoes dug into my heels. I'd wanted them for ages and had stood outside the shop window staring at them so many times, the assistants had started waving at me. Mum had bought them as a surprise – I knew she was trying to cheer me up – however, I couldn't wear them again as they would always remind me of today. I didn't want to, but I wondered which shoes Gran had on in the coffin.

Dad appeared. "You still sure you want to go?"

"Yes." I ignored the stabbing pain in my stomach that spread to my heart.

He came over to hug me, and Mum joined in, encircling us both with her arms, smelling of hairdryer-warm hair and freshly sprayed perfume. It was strange, her wearing *Deep Space Black*. Dad nicknamed her *the bird of paradise* – she loved brightly coloured clothing so much, Gran had always said it would be impossible to lose Mum in a crowd.

I wished we could have stayed hugging for the

whole day. And that I could have told them what had happened the morning Gran died. But I couldn't bear them hating me as much as I hated myself.

"Can you help me with this?" Mum asked Dad, letting go of us. She handed him her necklace. A small pair of *Lunar Silver* angel wings swung in the air as she faced the hallway mirror, lifting her hair out of the way. Dad's hands shook and it took him three goes to fasten the clasp. As she straightened the wings, a movement caught her eye. "Your gran is here," she said.

I whirled around, expecting her to be standing on the doorstep.

The hearse pulled up outside the gate.

I hadn't been inside the church since three Christmases ago. Gran had taken me to listen to the choir singing carols. Faces had glowed in the soft, flickering light of the candles and it smelled of polished wood, pine needles and cinnamon buns. I couldn't peel my eyes away from the stained-glass windows, which glowed like broken rainbows. I didn't know what the choir was singing about, but it sounded glorious, as if they were visiting us from another planet to make our hearts fly. The hairs on the back of my neck had stood on end and I'd shivered with delight, never wanting it to finish.

Today, the church was gloomy, and the pew hard. I could hear feet shuffling, people coughing and the creak of wood as they sat. The sun hid, making the stained-glass windows dull and lifeless.

I stared at a vase of flowers, sitting on a small table in front of me, and counted the number of *Glacier White* roses in it. And when I knew for certain how many there were, I gazed at my feet until my neck ached.

A large clatter made me turn. An old man had dropped a Bible and couldn't bend to pick it up. That's when I noticed everyone staring at me.

They all know it's your fault she's here.

I snapped my head round to the front, trying to ignore my thoughts. Gran smiled at me from the order of service pamphlet, as though we'd just shared a joke. My insides writhed like snakes in a cage.

I finally raised my eyes to look at what I'd been

avoiding since I'd entered the church. The coffin gleamed: all pale polished wood, shiny handles and *Empire Gold*–threaded cord with tassels. *Wings of Pegasus* flowers bloomed across the top of it: both beautiful and gut-wrenching at the same time.

I squirmed on the pew. If Mum and Dad knew it was my fault Gran had died, they'd never want anything to do with me again.

They'll send you to prison to be locked up. For ever.

The thought of losing them too made me suck in my breath. Dad studied my face to see if I was OK. I avoided his gaze, just in case what I had done showed in my eyes. Dad squeezed my arm and Mum handed me a tissue. I dabbed my face with it.

As the minister spoke about Gran, the words swirled above my head like a flock of startled birds. When everyone stood to sing her favourite hymns, my legs trembled and my throat shut.

I didn't want to say goodbye to Gran.

I would give anything to say sorry to her. *Anything.*

After the service, Dad led Mum and me outside. I

noticed an angel perched on top of one of the graves across from us. Its eyes were fearful and its hands clasped in prayer. How terrible to be frozen that way for ever and ever.

Even though the place was full of the living, I shivered.

Ties flapped, ladies held on to their hats and people blew their noses. Someone's tissue dropped and tumbled away to hide behind a bunch of lilies wrapped in plastic.

The minister said more words in a soothing voice.

I glared at him, angered by his calmness. I wanted to kick him so hard, tears would fill his eyes too.

Dad stepped forward to help lower Gran's coffin into the ground.

I glanced up at the sky. Gran and I had been planning to go on a galactic flight to space. I had asked her if we could visit the other side of the moon. She had answered we could, but we'd need to start saving our pennies because the price of the tickets was *astronaut-omical*. Dad had told her to stop filling my head with nonsense. She'd patted my knee and whispered anything was possible if you put your mind to it.

I heard six thuds as the flowers landed on top of the coffin. Dad offered me the rose he was about to throw in.

I stepped back, shaking my head. The trees spun and the blister on my heel burst.

The flower hit the wood and Dad returned to us. I buried my head in his coat. Mum grasped my hand. Tears salted my lips. Dad held me so tight, it was hard to breathe.

Gran had gone to the stars without me.

The Brigg Inn was covered in ivy on the outside and tartan on the inside. Gran had always enjoyed visiting here because the gardens were well-kept and the views over the river postcard-perfect. She always said the scenery was just as pleasant on the inside too because the waiters were very handsome, which made Dad tut and Mum laugh.

Nessie, Dodo and Margot were Gran's best friends. Dad called them *The Hustlers* – even though they had *New York City Winter* hair and smiled sweetly, they were ruthless at card games. Today, they fussed over me, eager I knew how much Gran had loved me. This made me feel so bad I thought I was going to be sick. They told me their favourite stories about her to cheer me up, but it was awful because Gran wasn't here to chip in. I smiled in the correct places, not wanting to upset them because they loved Gran too.

Mrs Shellycoat, the librarian, poured me a cup of tea. Gran and I thought she was great because she always knew what we were interested in reading, and sometimes she would slip us biscuits, even though there was a huge sign on the wall saying: *Please do not eat in the library.*

Mum was flitting from guest to guest with a tray of sandwiches. Dad was chatting to a man who had a stick and shouted when he spoke. Mum had said I could ask my best friend, Isla, along for company but her dad wouldn't let her take the day off school. It was probably just as well because she would have got bored and then done something like see how many mini sausage rolls she could cram into her mouth at the same time. Isla had texted me an emoji of a broken heart this morning. I'd not replied.

I found a spot in the corner, next to a sofa. As the sherry was passed around, the soft murmur of voices steadily grew into noisy chatter. I watched everyone for a while, wishing Gran was with me. She would have spotted Judy Heffton from the slimming club piling her plate high with sandwiches and rolled her eyes at Meredith Swift's hat, which was the same size as a flying saucer.

Miss Mirk loomed into view, clutching a giant handbag that was bashed and frayed at its edges. I didn't know it was possible my heart could sink even lower. Her hat was *Plum Fandango* coloured and had two feathers sprouting out from either side of it. They shimmered *Electric Rainforest* and waggled like insect antennae when she talked. The feathers were so beautiful, it was hard to tear my eyes away from them.

Miss Mirk stared at me. One of the arms was missing from her spectacles, and the lenses reminded me of empty shop windows that'd been smeared with cleaning products so you couldn't see properly into them.

I had to lean in close to hear what she was saying over the din.

"I know how you are feeling about your grandmother," she said. "I lost my beloved George years ago." Her hand fluttered to her throat. "The vet could not do anything for him."

I started counting to ten in my head. Dad told me it was a great way to stop yourself from saying something you'd later regret. As I reached fifteen, I still wanted to mutter two words that would make her eyes widen in shock.

Miss Mirk undid the clasp on her bag. I caught a glimpse of something black and furry inside it. She pulled out a sandwich and shoved it into her mouth. The side of the bag bulged and then flattened again.

"What were you doing peering into my garden yesterday?" she asked, crumbs spraying everywhere.

"My gran's cat is missing. I was searching for him."

"The black one with half a tail?" Miss Mirk wiped her nose on her sleeve.

"Yes."

"He evacuates his bowels in my plant pots,

terrorizes the seagulls and chases dogs along the street." Miss Mirk pursed her lips together so hard they turned paler than sheets.

"Do you know where he is?"

She avoided my gaze, her eyebrows arching higher than normal. "Indeed not." The bag shook so violently, her hand shot up to steady it. There were three scratch marks on her wrist. She must have had a disagreement with something which owned claws, and right at that very second, I was convinced it was God.

"Miss Mirk, thank you for coming along today. Could I tempt you to a sherry?" said Mum, lifting up a tray of *Amber Dusk* liquid-filled glasses.

"Mum, I think God is in Miss Mirk's handbag." I blurted it out before I could stop myself.

The glasses on the tray rattled as Mum's eyes dropped to the bag, which stayed perfectly flat and still.

Miss Mirk put a protective arm over the bag. "Your daughter is in dire need of help if she thinks our dear Lord himself is in here." She swiped a sherry off the tray, knocking it back in one go.

"My daughter is not taking the Lord's name in vain: the cat that is missing is called Godfrey. If Coral has in any way upset you, please accept my sincerest apologies. Godfrey disappearing is adding to our distress at what is already a difficult time for us all."

Miss Mirk grabbed another glass, drained it dry and belched.

Mum handed the tray to a passing waiter. "If you'd please excuse us, Miss Mirk." Hooking her arm under mine, Mum whisked me upstairs to the hotel lobby. It smelled of old leather, soot and air freshener.

The receptionist sat perfectly still, but her eyes followed us as we walked over to the fireplace, reminding me of a painting you'd expect to find hanging in a haunted house.

"What's going on?" Mum sounded dismayed.

"There was something black and furry in Miss Mirk's bag." I kicked at a stack of logs next to the fire.

Mum sighed in a way that indicated she was fast running out of energy. "Ladies sometimes keep odd things in their bags. What you saw will have been a scarf or something."

"Whatever it was, was alive."

Mum hesitated, her *Pearl Cloud* highlighter shimmered a thousand colours on her cheekbones as she tilted her head. "Has it been a bit too much? Do you want to go home?"

"You're not listening." I stamped my foot and the receptionist blinked.

The tone of Mum's voice changed from soft and patient to low and firm. "Let's say for a moment Miss Mirk has kidnapped God – which is highly unlikely because I'm assuming she hates cats – however, if she has, she wouldn't bring him here where he'd be right under our noses."

"She said God going missing was a blessing." I folded my arms in front of me.

"Miss Mirk is an unhappy lady who finds it easier to dislike things than to like them. In life, Coral, there are those who make you feel upbeat and light-hearted, and those who leave you feeling drained, as if they've stolen all your energy. Miss Mirk is one of those unfortunates."

"She's taken God because she *hates* him," I wailed.

Mum gave me *The Look* – the one that told me I was close to crossing a line I would regret going over. She massaged her right temple. "Remember when Dad shut God inside the car by accident? You could have heard his yowls for miles around. I know you are desperate to find him, but it couldn't have been him in her bag. Listen, you're tired and everything is going to feel really strange and out of sorts for the next while, and that's OK. We've all got to work through Gran's loss in our own way. However, this is not fair on Miss Mirk. Are you sure you don't want to go home? You could put on a film and curl up on the sofa? We won't be much longer here, I promise."

"I'll stay."

"Then take a stroll in the gardens and get some fresh air. Come and find me when it's safe for Miss Mirk to be in the same room as you. I'll have to go; your dad's signalling for me to rescue him from the cousins from Luncarty." Mum gave me a swift hug and sped off down the stairs.

I threw myself on to one of the leather chairs

facing the fire, which wasn't as comfortable as it looked. Hanging over the mantelpiece was an old painting of Guiltree Hill. Our class had gone there on a school trip last year. Mrs McHarpock had told us a witch was supposed to be buried under the huge boulder at the top of it. When I had asked her if the story was true, she got distracted by Justin Furic tripping up Peter Poker and muttered her life would be a lot easier if she could bury Justin Furic under the stone.

I slouched in the chair, my fingers tracing the cracks on its faded leather arms. The witch wasn't under the rock on Guiltree Hill. She was alive and well, in the hotel drinking sherry and called Miss Mirk.

What had that been in her handbag?

I heard the squeak of fingers gripping leather tightly. Miss Mirk stepped out from behind the chair. The *Electric Rainforest* feathers in her hat swayed as she hoisted her bag further up her shoulder. "You know what they say about curiosity – it killed the cat. Keep away from me and my property, or else." Miss Mirk stomped off towards the toilets.

The air thickened and the colour drained from my face.

Had she just threatened to murder God?

Laughter drifted up the stairs. The receptionist sprang to life as she answered the phone, her eyes boring into me as I fled out the door.

CHAPTER
4

I came to a halt outside the graveyard and peered over the wall. The one person who'd know how to get God home was lying silent in the ground.

I wiped the tears on my sleeve, sniffing hard. Gran used to bring me here when she visited Grandpa's grave. I had asked if she was ever afraid of the place. She'd laughed and told me the living were far more frightening than the dead. But the graveyard had always given me a funny feeling, as though someone was standing next to me, and sometimes I thought I saw strange lights out of the corners of my eyes.

The church sat quiet and watchful, the tip of its spire hidden in clouds. A robin flashed its *Bittersweet Autumn* breast as it landed on a sycamore branch and a magpie hopped sideways across the grass, rattling thuggishly. The wind made everything twitch except for the gravestones. There was a sadness in the air not even the breeze could chase away. It was as though everyone's grief hung about the place, lengthening shadows, mottling the stone and making the branches droop so low they almost touched the ground. The grass was covered in patches of *Natural Oak*. You would think it would be a *Lush Eden* with all the tears that must fall on it every day.

Gran's grave caught my eye.

Opening the gate, I walked up the path, trying not to jump as branches creaked, ribbons on bouquets fluttered or birds darted past me.

I settled myself beside Gran's headstone. A strip of *Bold Grasshopper* plastic grass had been placed over the grave and there was a fresh pile of earth to the side of it.

I knew Gran was next to Grandpa now, but she

should be with us at home, steaming up the kitchen windows cooking her leftovers soup, watching films with the volume at thirty-five, hiding from the Cleaneazier catalogue man or pinching my *Violet Drama* nail polish.

Mum said I wasn't to think about what I'd lost. She told me to remember the things about Gran that had made me happy. Except every time I did, I missed her a trillion times more and the splintered pieces of my heart stuck into my ribcage like needles.

Crossing my legs, I rested my chin on my hands.

When Gran used to bring me here, she'd pull up the weeds and lay down flowers. Not bought ones: sweet peas from our garden, which were Grandpa's favourite. The only time she'd be still was right before we left. I remembered how she would lean forward to touch the headstone and close her eyes, as if she was somehow telling Grandpa all her thoughts.

Maybe if I did the same I could talk to her?

My fingers traced over the black letters and numbers on the gravestone. The icy marble stole the warmth from my hand.

I closed my eyes, concentrating hard.

Gran?

I held my breath.

Gran? Are you there?

The trees shivered; a fallen leaf scraped across the path behind me.

I want you to know I think Miss Mirk has stolen God and I'm not sure what to do.

I pressed my palm flat against the stone.

What I really came here to tell you is how sorry I am for. . .

A hand touched my shoulder.

I cried out and scrambled to my feet, my skin prickling. "What do you think you're doing?" I yelled at the boy standing next to me.

His eyes widened as though it was me who had given *him* the surprise.

Anger ripped through my body faster than a wildfire. "Well?" I prayed he couldn't hear my heart thundering in my chest. I was, after all, alone in a graveyard with a strange boy.

He wore *Witching Hour Black* trousers, a long *Clockface*-coloured shirt and scuffed boots. His face was covered in freckles, reminding me of a page in a dot-to-dot puzzle book gone wrong. The boy's eyes were *Secret Garden Ivy* and his hair *Conker Harvest* with streaks of *Antique Silver* at his temples, though he must have been only a few years older than me.

I blinked twice.

He was glowing the same shade of *Celestial Spark* that Grandpa had when I'd spied him in the hallway.

I glanced towards the gate and then back at him. I was sure he hadn't been at the funeral; however, there had been so many people it was hard to tell.

"Can you see me?" he asked, gawping as if I was a stone angel that had just sprung to life.

I froze, unsure how to answer.

My eyes followed him as he ducked down and moved from side to side.

"Oh! You have no idea what this means – thank heavens I've found you! Please allow me to introduce myself. My name is Lyart... Where are my manners? My condolences for your loss..."

Something fizzed deep inside me and started to bubble up. Blood whooshed through my veins and my heart drummed in my ears. Words shot out of my mouth the same way lava spouts from a volcano.

"It's creepy sneaking up on girls in graveyards," I spat, before storming off towards the path.

"Wait! There are some important things I must tell you." I heard his footsteps as he pursued me. "It's a matter of life and death."

Today could not be over soon enough.

I fought hard not to break out into a run; the boy was even crazier than I'd thought. Not even Mr McCubbin, my physics teacher, was this weird. If I could just reach the gate, I'd be seconds away from the Brigg Inn and safety.

"You have no idea how long I've waited to find someone living to talk to!" Lyart caught up with me. "Coral, the first thing you need to know is the earthbound are spirits who have chosen not to cross over to heaven after death, but to remain here instead. Most people can't see them, but *you* can."

I stopped and whirled around. It was clear I was dealing with someone who was completely and utterly stark raving bonkers.

"The next thing you should know is your gran has chosen to become heavenbound and will leave the earth on the next full moon. This means she is still here and I can take you to her, if you wish to see her one last time."

I gasped, resisting the urge to ball up my fist and punch Lyart on the nose. "Who even are you?" Every part of me shook with rage.

"Ah, you're not good with names either. I always forget them, and you'd think being the Keeper of Halloway, I'd have special memory powers; sadly not. Allow me to introduce myself again. I'm Lyart," he said with a bow.

I ignored his answer. "Are you from my school? How do you know my name? Is this a wind-up?" I checked the trees and bushes for Justin Furic or any of the other boys.

Lyart raised his hands as though trying to reassure me. "I don't go to your school. I live here in Halloway churchyard. . ."

"Let me tell *you* something. What you are saying about taking me to see my gran . . . is beyond horrible . . . and you should be ashamed of yourself." My cheeks flushed *Amsterdam Tulip*.

Lyart's brows came down, puzzled. "Do you not want to talk to your gran again?"

My heart near exploded like a popped balloon. He'd just said the one thing I wanted to hear more than anything else, but no matter how much I wished it was true, it just wasn't possible. The cruelness of his lie stung worse than jellyfish.

"If you. Know what's good for you. You will *never* speak to me again." I didn't have enough breath in my body to say it in one sentence.

The gate to the graveyard squeaked open and I heard footsteps – a chance for me to make my escape. As I wiped my eyes, a familiar face came into view.

"Coral," said Dad. "I've been searching for you everywhere. Mum told me you were in the hotel gardens. You should have let us know you were in here."

I glared at Lyart, who stood at the side of the path.

"Are you OK?" asked Dad. "Mum said you had a run-in with Miss Mirk, today of all days." He hadn't even asked who the scruffy boy was.

"She was rude about God." I glared at Lyart, wishing he would go away.

"Miss Mirk upsets everyone. She's a professional *upsetterer*, if there's such a word," replied Dad.

"I'm certain she's kidnapped him." I slid my eyes back over to Dad.

"Your mum mentioned you thought you'd spotted God in Miss Mirk's handbag. She is many things, but I wouldn't have her down as a cat rustler."

Lyart distracted me by stepping out from the shadows and disappearing behind Dad.

"*What are you doing?*" I called out to Lyart, nervously.

Dad answered, thinking I was speaking to him. "I'm wondering if you're ready to go? Mum is taking Nessie, Margot and Dodo home. They've had a bit too much sherry and they're singing at the tops of their voices. Management at the hotel asked them to leave."

Without warning, Lyart walked clean through Dad's body – who didn't flinch once.

My jaw dropped.

"I know, shocking stuff getting chucked out of a hotel at a funeral." Dad rubbed his eyes. "Ach, I'm glad they let off some steam; they'll miss Gran as much as we will."

Dad couldn't see Lyart! He really couldn't!

Lyart strode towards the giant sycamore tree. "I wouldn't lie to you, Coral. I can take you to your gran, but only if you help me with a matter of utmost urgency first. Many lives are at risk, so I'll need an answer by tomorrow. I'm really hoping you'll say yes." Shafts of sunlight appeared, piercing through his body in *Melted Butter* spears.

"What are you gawping at?" asked Dad, following my gaze over to the tree.

"A robin! Thought I saw a robin." The truth was way too strange to try and explain.

Dad stuck his hands in his pockets. "Your gran always said if you saw a robin it was someone in the spirit world sending their love."

I glanced over at the tree but Lyart had gone.

Dad put his arm around my shoulders and leaned on me. "Come on, I think we deserve the power of pizza tonight."

The sun's dying rays turned the clouds *Gold Doubloon*, *Glazed Raspberry* and *Lavender Posey*.

As shadows reached out across the path, I bit my lip. Was it possible Lyart was telling the truth and I could see Gran one more time?

Foxes raided bins for food, owls swooped silent as bats, a dog barked at a cat chasing a mouse and seagulls gave their last cackles of the day as they wheeled above the rooftops. A sea breeze stirred, nudging the dozing trees awake. A satellite flashed past the stars and the shy moon hid behind *Silver Rocket* clouds. Leaves trembled and branches tapped against my window, but my eyes were already open. I knew Gran was dead, except I couldn't stop worrying that she'd be cold in her coffin. Even in the summertime, she'd feel chilled, which she'd always blamed on poor circulation. And God couldn't curl up in her lap to warm it any more.

I wiped my eyes. I hadn't even realized it was possible to cry silently until today. As if it hadn't been enough having to say goodbye to Gran. Had I actually seen a spirit boy? An *earthbound*, as he'd called it. I had watched Lyart walk through Dad;

could it have been a trick of the light? And what did he mean when he'd mentioned lives were at risk?

My insides churned as though I was on a waltzer ride at the fair. If he was fibbing about taking me to see Gran one last time, it would be the cruellest trick ever played on me. It was the one thing I wanted most in the world. My breath caught in the back of my throat as I imagined hugging her and telling her how sorry I was for what happened.

But how could any of this be possible?

The trees stirred and I heard a yowl outside. I got out of bed and padded over to the window. I peered into the garden but couldn't spot any dark shapes slinking across the lawn. I hoped God was safe wherever he was.

Something moved in the shadows and my eyes darted over to Miss Mirk's garden. She was hunched over a bin bag, dragging it up the stairs. Whatever was inside it was heavy. With one last heave, she staggered through her doorway, the bin bag vanishing from view. The glass on the door rattled as she slammed it shut.

What was she smuggling into her house at this time of night?

My heart raced faster than the second hand on my alarm clock as I jumped back into bed. No wonder Miss Mirk didn't want me poking my nose in her business; she was definitely up to no good. Why would she kidnap God if she hated animals? None of it made sense and I couldn't talk to Mum and Dad about it because they didn't believe there had been anything strange in her handbag. The question was: how could I prove Miss Mirk had stolen God? As I lay staring up at the ceiling, I shivered every time a radiator clanked or a floorboard creaked.

CHAPTER 5

Dad and I held the poster up for Mum to inspect. She was sitting at the breakfast table in her dressing gown, halfway through her fourth yawn, which made me yawn too. I'd been awake most of the night as well.

"It's a really good picture of God and the letters are nice and big, so people will be able to read them as they are driving past in their cars, too. Who chose the colour?" asked Mum.

"Me." I was certain colours could be lucky or unlucky. Although the Chinese believe red brings good fortune, Gran swore it wasn't so advantageous for Mrs McHugh at the curling club because it brought out the broken veins on her face. Gran said they were *gin blossoms*, except I have no idea what those even are. Whenever I'd worn something *Peppermint Leaf*, I'd always had the best day. I'd read at the library that green was sacred to Egyptians because it gave them hope, so that's why I'd chosen it for God's poster. *Peppermint Leaf* might not work for me any more; however, I was sure it would for him and that seeing his picture would jog the memory of a neighbour who might have spotted him in Miss Mirk's garden and then Mum and Dad would believe me that she'd kidnapped him. We had decided to write his full name under his photo because Dad said if we just put *God is Missing*, we might upset the minister who lived nearby, or spark a huge *philosophical debate* in the neighbourhood.

Dad insisted it would be a good idea to join Saltbay's Lost Pets page on Facebook. We had scrolled through it and found missing dogs, cats, guinea pigs, rabbits, budgies and even a parrot. Nip, the dog from the poster, was there too, which meant he couldn't have been found yet. Seeing all the photos of the animals at home, in happier times, made me sad and more determined than ever to find God. I'd do anything to get him back here with us where he belonged.

I grabbed a bowl and emptied the last of the cereal into it. I sat and watched the milk changing *Cocoa Disco*. Dad made a coffee and scrolled through the emails on his phone. He never normally spoke until he'd finished his first cup of the day.

"Your dad and I have to go to the lawyers this morning to discuss some important things to do with your gran." Mum buttered some toast and took a bite. "Will you be OK here for a while?"

Mum and Dad had agreed I could take the week off school. I knew if someone asked what had happened or mentioned they were sorry to hear my news, I'd just burst into tears. And my mind was way too distracted to pay attention in class anyway.

"Can I put the posters up?" I raised my eyebrows.

Mum and Dad glanced at each other. Dad shrugged and Mum placed her toast on her plate.

"I'll stay on Our Street and Brown Street." Brown Street wasn't actually called Brown Street but for some reason dog owners never scooped up the poop there, so Dad and I renamed it. We'd given all the nearby streets, lanes and cul-de-sacs new titles: something which had kept us both endlessly amused and made Mum and Gran shake their heads.

"What I don't tape to trees and lamp posts, I'll pop through people's doors," I added.

A thought occurred to me. If I put one through Miss Mirk's door, I could peer through the letter box to see if I could spot any signs God was there. I leaned forward on the table, crumbs crunching under my elbows. "The sooner people know God is missing the better."

"Will you take your phone with you?" Dad asked.

I nodded.

"Is it switched on and fully charged?" He narrowed his eyes at me.

"It is." I gave an exaggerated blink.

"Will you promise only to stick to Our Street and Brown Street? And not to go into someone's house even if they offer you a brand-new seasonal paint chart of autumnal hues from Homeworld?"

"This is serious," said Mum, glowering at Dad.

"I promise," I said quickly, before she could change her mind.

"Well then, you can go, but if you break any of the aforementioned rules, you're grounded for the rest of your life and into the afterlife too." Dad set his face in a stern expression.

I thought about what Lyart had said. I wished I could tell Mum and Dad what had taken place in the graveyard, except there was no way they would believe me – especially not after they thought I was making it up about Miss Mirk kidnapping God. And no matter how desperate I was to see Gran to tell her how sorry I was for what happened, I knew deep down inside it just wasn't possible. I'd been mad even listening to Lyart in the first place. My insides crumbled as anger pulsed through my body. I ought to go straight round to the graveyard and thump him for lying to me.

The clouds zipped across the sky, in a hurry to reach the next town. The cool air smelled fresh and of the sea. Saltbay beach was only a ten-minute walk from the house; Gran and I loved going there on days just the same as this. The waves would be *Mermaid's*

Tail tipped with galloping *Chalk White* horses, which would thunder on to the sand, leaving behind gifts of glossy seaweed, driftwood, bright plastics, smashed crabs, and a rainbow of broken shells. If the wind was strong, jellyfish would roll in on the tide and lie still, gleaming like giant milky opals. Swallows swooped after flies faster than thoughts and wagtails would flutter and bob amongst scratchy patches of dried seaweed. As much as I would have loved the breeze to chase away my sadness for a while, walking along the sand without Gran would feel as weird as the ocean not being there.

I tugged on my *Squid Ink* beanie hat, buttoned up my *Heartthrob Red* coat and tied a knot in my *Sweet Apple* scarf. I hurried out on to the street, attaching posters to all the lamp posts. That's when I noticed Miss Mirk's gate was already open. After checking the coast was clear, I nipped up her path, ignoring the nerves helter-skeltering around my insides.

I watched the net curtains for movement, but they stayed stock-still.

Striding up the three steps to her door, I took off my rucksack and pulled the posters out. I knelt on the mat and opened the brass letter box. It was stiff, so I pushed it hard, the tip of my finger turning *Ballerina Gown*. The poster landed on the other side of the door and slid across the dark wooden floor. My eyes took a minute to adjust to the gloom. The hallway was painted *Dragon Blood* and the pictures on the walls were squint, as if someone had brushed past them in a hurry. I spied scratches on the doors, which didn't mean much because it was an old house. Gran always said the more marked something was, the more interesting a story it had to tell. I studied the shadows for God, but he wasn't there, so I held my breath and strained my ears for any yowling or hissing.

"What are you doing?" said a quiet voice behind me.

The letter box snapped shut as I scrambled to my feet, letting go of all the posters. They fluttered down the steps, catching in the towering dandelions and knee-high nettles.

"Not content with spying on me again, you are now littering my flower beds." Miss Mirk's eyes glinted *Pewter Dagger*.

I chased after the posters, retrieving them from the weeds as quickly as I could.

"Miss Mirk, I wasn't sure if you were home or not. Can I give you one of these?" I straightened up and passed her a poster, my cheeks flushing *Bullseye* with the lie.

She wasn't wearing her glasses so held it away from her at arm's length. The brooch pinned to her lapel caught my eye. It was *Chiffon White* with three talons on it and very much looked like a bird's foot.

"Nature has not been kind to this animal; it is a brute of a cat." She sniffed, her nose whistling.

"Pardon me?"

"I take it you have not located it yet?"

I remembered Mum's warning about being polite. "No, Miss Mirk; we've not found *him* yet. That's why I'm handing out posters in case he's been spotted . . . nearby."

"I told you to stay away from me and my property. I will not warn you again." Miss Mirk crumpled the poster into a ball and stuffed it inside her handbag. She brushed past me and heaved her shopping trolley up the front steps. One of its wheels caught and the flap flew open. Four cans spilled out, bounced down the steps and rolled towards my feet. To my astonishment, they were tins of cat food.

Miss Mirk charged after them, her face changing from *Macaroon Cream* to *Blushing Vixen*.

My anger started in the pit of my stomach and then travelled through my veins, reaching every single part of my body. It was so strong, my heart shrank behind my ribs and skipped some beats.

"If this food is for God and you're keeping him from me or you've harmed him in any way. . ."

Miss Mirk cut me short. "No wonder your grandmother wound up in an early grave. Stay away from me." She opened her door, bumped the trolley inside and slammed it shut behind her. Some chips of paint floated to the ground like dirty confetti.

She knows it's your fault Gran's dead.

The cloud above snagged on a jagged TV aerial and burst. Rain started to fall.

Fleeing from her garden, I tore past my house.

I sprinted so fast birds flapped, dogs barked and people stared behind me, curious of what I was running from.

CHAPTER
6

I shot through the gate, dashing across the squelchy grass towards the giant sycamore tree. Water seeped in through my high-tops and the *Golden Spice* curls that poked out beneath my beanie hat had darkened to *Espresso*.

Falling seeds the same shape as helicopter blades whirled down on to the ground. The graveyard spun and I could no longer breathe. I collapsed, gasping for air.

Miss Mirk knows Gran's dead because of you. How long before she tells Mum and Dad?

My thoughts emptied my lungs and I wheezed.

"Slow your breathing, Coral. Inhale through your nose ... that's it ... hold it ... hold it... OK, you can exhale out through your mouth now. You're going to be fine – again. Breathe in through your nose."

I squeezed my eyes shut and listened to Lyart's voice. When my lungs finally filled, I sat up.

"An old friend of mine, Will, used to have asthma. It's something I've never forgotten." Lyart checked his pocket watch, which reminded me of something you'd see in a period drama on TV. "What you had was a panic attack and they're usually triggered by fear."

I pushed all thoughts of Miss Mirk out of my mind in case I ended up gasping, round-mouthed, like a fish out of a pond.

Inching away from Lyart, I rested my back against the tree. Even though he'd made me feel better, it didn't mean I trusted him.

"I wasn't expecting you back so soon," he commented.

I glanced over at Gran's gravestone. I missed her

so much my heart felt as though it had been flattened by a steamroller. I brought my knees up, hugging them. "So how did you do that thing when you walked through my dad yesterday? Some kind of trick?"

"I'm earthbound, but I'm still technically a ghost."

"Has anyone told you that you have serious issues with lying? If fibbing about taking me to see my gran before she crosses over to heaven wasn't enough, now you're pretending you're something out of *Ghostbusters*?"

Lyart straightened himself up. In a flash, he disappeared into the trunk of the sycamore tree and then stuck his head out the side of it, waving at me.

As I leapt to my feet in a panic, he appeared at my side.

"I didn't mean to frighten you, Coral! I just wanted you to know I'm telling you the truth. I can explain everything but we can't talk here." I could tell from his eyes it was important I believed him.

"W-why me?" I stammered. "Why can I see ghosts?"

"Ghosts are off the usual light spectrum, Coral – our colour can't be picked up by the living. It's probably for the best; imagine being able to see the dead everywhere you turn? But you ... you saw me straight away. You must be able to detect a whole range of colours others can't."

I pictured all the paint charts on my walls at home.

"Is there anything unusual about me?" Lyart tilted his head, waiting for an answer.

His skin shone as though there was a faint halo around it. Exactly the same as Grandpa's when he had appeared.

My shoulders slumped. "There's a weird thing going on – you're sort of glowing *Celestial Spark*," I said begrudgingly.

Lyart gave me a triumphant smile.

"Is Grandpa here?" I asked.

"He crossed over to heaven when you moved in with your gran because he knew she'd be in good company."

I squinted at the headstones. "How come there are no other ghosts? It is a graveyard, after all."

"There's something in here that has sent them all into hiding," Lyart whispered, his eyes furtive.

I snorted. "So now you're telling me ghosts get scared?"

"They feel exactly the same emotions as when they were alive – especially when they are in danger."

A *Candy Apple* leaf fell from above, landing next to me. "How come people choose to be earthbound ghosts anyway? Why doesn't everyone just go to heaven?"

"Lots of different reasons; they could be earthbound because they want revenge for an injustice. Many are too scared to cross over to the unknown and others refuse to leave their loved ones behind. I'm earthbound because I'm the Keeper of this graveyard."

I frowned. "What does that mean?"

"It's my job to protect both the living and the dead from those who wish them harm. Come on, we need to get moving. There is much we need to discuss and time is against us." Lyart headed off.

"Where are you going?" I called after him.

He pointed over to a small headstone covered in *Salsa Red* lichen.

"A *grave*?"

"Coral, if you want to be reunited with your

gran, you're going to have to trust me, but we need to hurry."

I stared at Lyart. His eyes weren't shifty or avoiding mine; there was a warmth and kindness in them. And part of me was desperate to believe he really was telling the truth about Gran. My heart leapt the same way as a salmon up a stream at the thought of seeing her again.

I brought out my mobile. "I've got this, just in case. It's a phone and if I push these buttons, my mum will be here in seconds and she's scary when she's angry."

Lyart's face fell. "I've noticed, if I stand too close to someone with a *phone*, they stop working, which must be a terrible inconvenience judging by the language used when it happens."

Even though the mobile had been fully charged before I left the house, the battery had just died. I pressed some keys in vain. Mum and Dad were going to ground me for the rest of my life if they called.

"Coral, I have no interest in harming you; I need your assistance," said Lyart solemnly. "All I ask is you hear me out in private: this place has eyes, ears and a whole lot more besides."

His hand hovered over some carvings on the front of the gravestone. His finger pushed a woman's face frozen in a scream, then a skull and lastly, a strange bird.

Lyart spun around to face me. "Word of caution, Coral. If I tell you to run, do exactly that. The only place you will be safe is outside the graveyard walls."

Before I could say another word, a rectangular hole appeared in the grass, and Lyart leapt down some stairs.

My mouth opened and closed.

I took one last look at the graveyard and followed him into the dark.

I could smell damp soil, mouldering leaves and a sharp odour I didn't recognize. The narrow corridor sloped downwards at a steep angle and everything was *Crow Black*. My chest felt tight again, as though invisible arms were squeezing me, and I struggled to take a breath.

Just as I decided it would be a smart idea to leave, a hand gripped my elbow.

"Coral, I'm sorry, you've not been here before and

it's bound to be alarming." Lyart led me around a corner into a wider passageway. Thousands of *Ivory Dazzle* dots twinkled high above on the ceiling.

"Are they stars?" I asked.

"Glow-worms."

"Do you use them to find your way around in here?"

"No, we have glamps."

"What are they?"

"In my world, there are good and bad spirits. It's always best to trap the bad ones because they can make you feel poorly or angry. In extreme cases, they can even be destructive, so they are much better off doing something useful like lighting our way. Here's one now."

A hollow had been made in the wall. In it sat a clear glass ball with a bright *Rebel Blue* light streaking around inside. It stopped when it saw us, and an angry face peered out. I stepped back in fright.

"As soon as the blue light turns white, it means the bad spirit has changed into good energy, which can be released." Lyart tapped the side of the glass.

"It'll then zoom above ground to find someone in the graveyard who is sad, so it can make them feel better for a while. It's often the reason people take great comfort from visiting the dead."

I noticed the walls flashing and twinkling. On closer inspection, they were covered in brooches, hat pins, buttons, earrings, gold teeth, tie pins, necklaces, pendants, hair clasps, lockets, watches, bracelets and diamond rings.

"The dead can't take their belongings with them and they are of no use to the earthbound; however, they serve as a reminder we were all once flesh and blood." He raced down some steps and I followed, ducking under a mass of tangled tree roots dangling from the ceiling that looked like a giant clump of veins.

Lyart tore along a corridor with doors on either side of it. The glamps flickered every shade of blue imaginable, and for a moment, I could have believed I was at the bottom of the sea.

"Here we are!" He passed straight through a closed wooden door and vanished. I wondered how long it would take Lyart to notice I wasn't right behind him.

"So, you're the one he's been going on and on about," said a voice.

Startled, I checked behind me, except there was no one there. Was I hearing another ghost?

"Up here, shorty."

Above the door was a *Fire Brick* sandstone gargoyle which puffed air from its nostrils and waggled its horns. The gargoyle had the kind of face that could turn your hair *Moonshine*.

Staggering back, I slammed into the wall. My eyes must be playing tricks on me! Had it really just spoken?

The gargoyle watched me with interest. That was when I noticed its fangs.

I shuffled away from it.

"Oi! Where are you off to? You've only just got here," said the gargoyle.

Lyart came flying out from his door. "Coral! It's OK. Moonzy won't harm you, she's a friend of mine."

Unsure what to think, I hesitated.

Lyart stepped towards me. "Let me introduce you. Coral, this is Moonzy. Moonzy, meet Coral."

Moonzy's nostrils flared. "Coral as in the reef?"

I gawped at the gargoyle and swallowed. "As in the colour," I replied.

Lyart caught Moonzy's eye. "Let me know if you hear anything. Coral, this way, please."

Following Lyart into the room, I scooted past Moonzy as fast as I could. "How is it even possible a gargoyle can talk?" I muttered as Lyart ushered me in.

"Everything you can imagine is real here," he replied. "Speaking gargoyles, witches, moss goblins, burrowing nim-nims, you name it."

"Are you seriously telling me witches exist?" I forgot to close my mouth.

Lyart glanced at me as though I was daft. "They fly around the sky most nights."

I stood, waiting for him to laugh, but nothing happened. I sighed. I was in a chamber underneath a graveyard with a ghost and a gobby gargoyle. Perhaps there could be witches in the world too. I remembered what Mrs McHarpock had said about the one that was supposed to be buried under the boulder at Guiltree Hill. Maybe there was a grain of truth in it, after all.

I twirled around in a circle on the spot. The room was narrow, with a ceiling so high that I couldn't actually see it. Lots of framed portraits hung on the walls and a rickety pile of coffins was stacked in the corner.

The *Dream White* and *Rebel Blue* glamps gave the room an eerie glow.

Lyart sat himself behind an ornately carved desk and gestured towards a stone bench opposite it. "Please, make yourself comfortable."

The bench was cold and hard, reminding me of the church pew at Gran's funeral. I shook the thought from my head. "Where are we?"

"This is my family's burial plot."

I crossed my arms. "You said you keep the living and the dead safe, but what are you protecting them from?"

Moonzy stuck her head inside the door to hear his reply.

"Grave robbers, body snatchers, flesh creepers, baneshanks, groaner goblins, floods, earthquakes, rat swarms and a relatively new threat called property developers."

I pulled off my hat, trying to take everything in.

Lyart cleared his throat. "I need you to listen carefully to what I'm about to tell you. On the same evening as Halloween, a Hallow moon is going to appear in the sky. It's a rare event that only happens once every two hundred years. The moon's light is so bright it can guide all those who wish to go, over to heaven. It also allows the living to reunite with their loved ones before they leave for good."

"Are you saying I'd be able to speak to my gran?" I asked, glancing up at Moonzy, who nodded.

The thought of seeing her face other than in a photo or a memory made my heart ache. I would hug her so tight and tell her how much I loved her.

What if she doesn't want to talk to you? What if she blames you for what happened?

My thoughts triggered a wave of sadness that crashed through my body, crushing my heart against my ribcage. I squeezed my eyes shut and started to sob.

Lyart leapt up, alarmed. "Please don't upset yourself. So very few ever get a chance such as this." I heard him stride across the floor; a cold draught let me know he'd returned to my side.

He was holding a glamp so radiant, you could have believed a star was trapped inside it. An angelic face smiled out at me through the glass, its rays turning my tears *Sparkle Festival*.

Lyart pressed the glamp. The spirit shot out of the glass and rattled the lids of all the coffins. It zoomed all the way to the top of ceiling and I gasped as hundreds of cobwebs lit up like neon signs. Without warning, the light sped towards me, faster than a meteorite, and vanished straight into my ear.

My eyes widened in shock.

"Better now?" Lyart peered closely at me.

Pressure began to build up inside me. The skin on my arms bubbled with goosebumps.

I jumped to my feet. "What's happening?"

"Ah! You've lots of bad thoughts trapped inside you. Let them go," Lyart said, keeping his voice calm.

"I don't know how!" I shrieked when I saw the lumps on the palms of my hands.

Moonzy called over to me. "Coral, relax and start imagining all negative thoughts or feelings leaving you."

I closed my eyes. I had been a fool to trust Lyart.

I was stuck deep under the ground and fast becoming a roll of bubble wrap. All of a sudden, Gran's picture on the order of service pamphlet from the funeral floated into my mind and lumps erupted over my neck and cheeks.

"Do you have a special place; somewhere that always makes you feel happy? Think, Coral! Think!" Moonzy squealed.

I imagined the sun warming my skin. My nose filled with the breath of the sea and I heard the familiar sound of waves breaking on to the shore. Gran's laughter swirled around me and the sand shifted under the soles of my feet.

My jaws unclenched.

A loud pop made my eyes fly open and a voice cursed in my ear.

"Thank heavens you didn't explode, Coral!" Lyart clasped his hands together, greatly relieved. "What you are hearing are your bad thoughts."

One by one, the bubbles on my skin burst and the room filled with grumbles, curses, moans and whining.

"I once heard similar language that time those

awful pirates got lost in here." Moonzy flattened her horns.

As rapidly as the voices had shown up, they left, taking all my troubles with them.

No more horrible thoughts clouded my mind, pinched at my stomach or sat heavy on my shoulders. My heart floated, weightless, the same way an astronaut does in space.

I beamed at Lyart and Moonzy.

"What did you think about?" said Moonzy, eager to hear my answer.

"Saltbay beach."

"That's the first time I've seen you smile, Coral. It suits you," said Lyart.

I laughed. "I feel tingly and . . . brilliant."

Lyart rifled through one of the drawers in the desk, and handed me a test tube which had a stopper in it. The sides of the glass were decorated with *Sonic Silver* stars and planets.

"It's beautiful." I turned it over in my hands, mesmerized by the glittering constellations.

"It's a tear catcher," he said. "I'm afraid I don't have any hankies."

"A tear catcher? Seriously?"

"It's Victorian," added Moonzy.

"There will come a time it'll be of use to you," Lyart said.

"Well, thank you." I thought it best to accept it because it was the second time Lyart had made me feel better today. I slid the tear catcher into my pocket.

"Coral, I will only reunite you with your gran on the condition you help me with something first."

I sat forward on the bench.

"I'm afraid what I'm going to say will be extremely upsetting." Lyart paused. "For a very long time Halloway graveyard has held a secret. A dark entity has been held captive here for nearly two hundred years, against his will. He's earthbound, the same as me, and his name is Muckle Red . . . but he's also known as the Heart Collector." Lyart's gaze was steely.

Moonzy spoke, her voice thin and fragile. "When he was alive, he was responsible for the deaths of innocent children in Saltbay."

"Each time he took a life. . ." Lyart paused, his

face pained. "He stole the heart of his victim to keep as a trophy."

I was shocked something so gruesome had happened right here in Saltbay.

Moonzy's head and wings drooped, making her appear less fearsome.

Lyart stood and paced, agitated, his hands clasped behind him. "Word soon spread through the town that the Heart Collector walked amongst them and no child was safe. Rumours were rife: neighbours and families turned on each other. Bewildered and angry, the village concluded the deaths must be the work of black magic and hunted down as many of the local witches as they could." Lyart paused. "They were captured, found guilty without a fair trial and burned at the stake."

The glamps in the room dimmed, making shadows creep along the floor and walls towards us. A coolness settled on my skin; my body juddered as I shivered.

"Most of the witches fled for their lives, apart from one who stayed behind, determined to find out who was behind the killings. She stole a child from the local orphanage, padlocked her in a cage as bait and waited in the woods. It wasn't long before the child's cries attracted the attention of Muckle Red. He wore a chain of hearts and the witch knew without doubt she'd caught the real culprit. Seeking revenge for the deaths of her sisters, the witch put Muckle Red to sleep with a potion, brought him to Halloway graveyard and sealed him inside a coffin. A spell was cast so his spirit would be earthbound and trapped, unable to leave the grounds. However, there was a glitch in the magic – if Muckle Red could gather three special objects before the Hallow moon vanished at midnight, he'd walk free."

"If he escaped, what would happen?" I asked.

"Being trapped in here has not quelled his desire to inflict pain and misery; if anything it's made him worse. If the Heart Collector flees, he will once again stalk children, not just in Saltbay, but wherever he goes." Lyart's *Celestial Spark* glow faded.

A murderer roaming around the town was a terrifying thought. Isla and all my other friends could be in danger! The walls closed in; fear had once again found its way back to me.

"We're sorry, Coral," said Moonzy. "All this must be extremely difficult for you to take in."

I raised my eyes. "What happened to the witch?"

Lyart pulled his chair out and sat. "She was captured, but of course the deaths had now stopped because Muckle Red had been imprisoned in the graveyard. The people of Saltbay rejoiced, mistaking her for the Heart Collector, and she lost her life because of this." Lyart stared directly at me. "Muckle Red has only four days left to free himself. If he fails to collect the objects, the spell that has trapped him here will destroy him at the stroke of midnight, on the night of the Hallow moon."

"What are the objects he needs?" I looked from Lyart to Moonzy.

"Witch's tears, cannibal bones and a wrecker bird," answered the gargoyle.

I was sorry I had asked. What even was a wrecker bird?

Gripping on to the bench, I steadied myself. "You mentioned Muckle Red can't leave the graveyard, so won't that make it impossible for him to find them?"

75

"He'll bribe someone else to do the job for him, except he'll need to choose wisely. I've heard a hummock goblin and a whirlpool sprite have already tried on his behalf and failed."

"You said that if I helped you with something you'd take me to see my gran. What do you want me to do?"

"If you gather the witch's tears, cannibal bones and wrecker bird before anyone else, we can keep them safe from Muckle Red and make sure that he's finished off for good on the night of the Hallow moon. No child will ever lose their life to him again," Lyart said, his eyes wide and pleading.

"You want *me* to do that?" There was no way I could be trusted to keep a whole town of children safe by attempting to find a bunch of weird objects. And if others had tried and failed, what chance did I have?

I blanched *White Dove*.

"My best friend, Will, died because of Muckle Red. The grief his family and friends suffered has been a heavy burden for me to carry. Muckle Red didn't only steal hearts, he snuffed out lives, dreams and futures – and I can't let this tragedy happen to others." Lyart's hands trembled; he moved them out of sight, under his desk. "Will was the reason I chose to become the Keeper."

Moonzy sniffed, dabbing at her eyes with a wing.

"Can't *you* collect the objects?" I shifted on my seat.

"I would give anything to be able to do it, but once you become the Keeper, it's impossible to leave the graveyard." Lyart's voice was tinged with regret. "In fact, none of the ghosts here can."

"Except for me because I'm a poltergeist!" piped up Moonzy. "The only thing is, I've not left Halloway for two hundred years, and I'm worried I'll be thrown by what now exists outside these walls. You wouldn't be, though, Coral, and that could give us the advantage we need over Muckle Red."

Shame prickled my scalp. "I'm sorry. I'm not the right person for this. I'm useless at everything apart from drawing – I'm scared stiff of the dark and I think if I ever saw a witch for real, I'd faint."

I thought about Gran and how it was my fault she was no longer alive. "You need a person who's brave – not someone who's hopeless and who'll just let you down," I whispered.

Lyart rose and wandered over to one of the alcoves, where he picked up a small *Rebel Blue* glamp. The spirit inside butted its head against the glass. "In all the time I've been here, not one single other living person has noticed me. You're the only one who can help us, Coral."

Gran's coffin in the church flashed into my mind.

"I'm not who you think I am," I said. "I did something bad." I squirmed at hearing it said out loud for the first time.

Lyart studied my face for a while before finally speaking. "It's not what we've done wrong that makes us who we are, it's what we do to make it better."

His words hung in the air between us.

I picked my hat up from my lap. Gran had knitted it for me to keep me warm while I waited for the school bus in the mornings. She used to say every small act of kindness strengthened the soul.

My eyes watered as I pictured her face.

Muckle Red being a danger to children once again in Saltbay was unthinkable. The Heart Collector terrified the living daylights out of me, and four days to find these gruesome objects sounded utterly impossible – except if I didn't even try, I'd lose the one chance I had to see Gran to put things right with her.

I chewed on my lip. "You really think I could do all this given there's no time whatsoever?"

Lyart's eyes shone bright. "Moonzy would assist you."

The gargoyle nodded so hard, earth cascaded down from the ceiling. Something caught her attention and her head disappeared out the door. All of a sudden, she hissed, *"Muckle Red alert. Muckle Red alert."*

Lyart seized my rucksack and hauled me over to the door. "If Muckle Red suspects we are plotting against him, things will get dangerous, and I have less to lose than you: I'm already a ghost."

From the depths of the passageway, I could hear the sound of rushing air. The room trembled and lightning-shaped cracks inched their way up the walls. The *Rebel Blue* lights in the glamps whirled frantically.

"Can you remember the way out?" Moonzy squinted her eyes, trying to see into the gloom.

Horror trickled like melted ice cubes through my veins. I pulled on my hat and took the rucksack from Lyart, who clasped his hands over mine. "Will you help us?"

My heart thundered louder than a storm.

"Lyart! We can't risk Muckle Red catching her with us," interrupted Moonzy.

"Come back tonight with your answer – please say yes. We'll be waiting for you in the graveyard."

"We'll do our best to distract him. Remember, it's not safe until you are outside the walls." Moonzy flapped her wings. "Go!"

I shot along the corridor. The air dropped in temperature, changing my breath into milky clouds. If only I wasn't so far underground: I longed to see the trees and the sky, and to feel the rain on my skin again.

Something stirred and I glanced over my shoulder. My foot caught on a root and I stumbled forward, losing my balance. The tear catcher flew out of my pocket and rolled away. I patted the earth, searching for it. My hand hit something smooth and I picked it up, only to find it was an old finger bone. I stifled a yell and dropped it.

Gritting my teeth, I leapt up and sprinted forward, kicking an object that spun over to the wall, snagging on a tangle of roots. It was the tear catcher! I grabbed it and headed to the end of the tunnel. In front of me were three entranceways. One wrong turn could mean I may never escape from here. My chest tightened as I walked a few paces forward and picked the nearest one. Something growled up ahead in the dark, so I crept backwards, slower than a snail. That was when I caught a glimpse of earthen steps in the middle passage. These must have been the same ones Lyart and I came down! I bolted up them, relieved the walls were covered in jewellery, silently twinkling like man-made stars.

There it was again. A noise as if something large was gathering speed.

Zooming along the corridor with the high ceiling, I panted up the steep slope. The walls narrowed and spiders inched forward on to their webs, wondering if dinner had just arrived.

I reached the stairway which led to the graveyard, only to find the opening had vanished. I pushed against the solid ceiling of earth until my elbows hurt, but nothing gave way. I spun round, spotting something *Timeless White* under the mud on the wall, and started raking at it with my fingernails. Bit by bit, I uncovered the arm bones of a skeleton. I prodded it, gingerly, and waggled it from side to side.

The glamps grew more luminous. Faces appeared in them, baring their teeth. Tears welled up in my eyes and the tree roots gleamed as icicles formed on them.

I wrinkled my nose, grasped the skeleton's hand in mine and yanked it down the same way as the arm on a slot machine. The ceiling rumbled and my ears filled with the noise of stone grinding against stone. Daylight flooded in and I scrambled blindly up the last of the stairs. The rain fell hard and the headstones peeped out from behind a mist. I sprinted along the path, which shone *Treacle Black*. I could spy the wall ahead – the way to safety. With every last ounce of energy I possessed, I hurtled towards the gate. Just as I was flying through it, a hand caught me by the back of my coat and pulled me into the graveyard.

"Not so fast, young lady," said a voice.

I cried out with the fright of it.

CHAPTER
7

"Where have you been?" Mum asked in a way that was both concerned and angry at the same time.

Dad answered for me. "I found her in the graveyard, of all places."

Mum stared at me as though I was a puzzle she had no idea how to solve.

I caught sight of myself in the hallway mirror. My *Squid Ink* hat was on squint and my *Heartthrob Red* coat and *Sweet Apple* scarf were covered in dirt. There were rips in my houndstooth leggings and my high-tops were more mud than canvas.

"Take those off and leave them at the door. Go get changed and then come straight down; we have a visitor." Mum gave me *The Look*. I'd crossed over the line.

Dad had barely said two words to me in the car on the way home. He'd cursed every time the traffic lights turned *Poppy Harvest* and his knuckles had whitened gripping the steering wheel. You'd think if he had been the least bit worried, he'd be happy I'd been found safe and well.

I changed into another pair of houndstooth leggings and a *Watermelon Burst* hoody, wondering who could be downstairs.

I hoped Muckle Red hadn't harmed Moonzy or Lyart. The thought of him wanting to kill children for their hearts made me feel sick.

Here, in my room, surrounded by all my colours, it would be easy to believe this morning had all been a bad dream. I pulled out the tear catcher from my pocket and knew for certain: this whole nightmarish world really did exist. No matter how much Lyart needed me, there was no way I'd be able to find witch's tears, cannibal bones and a wrecker bird. I'd just let him down, Muckle Red would escape and I'd be responsible for the loss of more lives.

I hid the tear catcher in my rucksack, and tried to rid my mind of all thoughts about Muckle Red as I plodded down the stairs. I stood for a second with my hand resting against the lounge door. This was where Gran would always read her newspaper, which made her tut, grumble and sigh. And when I'd pointed this out to her, she'd informed me that bad news gave us the fire we needed in our bellies to change the world for the better.

Opening the door, I stopped dead in my tracks.

"Hello, Coral," said Miss Mirk.

It took all my strength to walk further into the room.

She must be here to tell them what you did on the day Gran died.

My swallow caught in my throat.

Mum was perched on the edge of her seat, her cup of tea untouched, and Dad's foot tapped on the floor as if he was listening to a fast tune on the radio.

If Miss Mirk had said something, they'd be yelling at me.

Mum's voice was spikier than thistles. "Coral, sit down."

Miss Mirk slurped her cup of tea and helped herself to a biscuit, as though she was settling down to watch her favourite TV programme. She was wearing a *Galapagos Green* hat which had a stuffed finch perched on the side of it. Every time she moved, it pecked the top of her head.

"Miss Mirk told us she caught you spying through her letter box this morning." Mum folded her arms in front of her.

"I was—"

"Don't interrupt."

I stared at Dad to see if he would stick up for me, but he avoided my gaze.

They didn't want me to speak; I was here to listen. I grabbed a cushion and hugged it.

"She also mentioned you were extremely rude. Not only did you not offer her a hand with her shopping trolley up the steps, but when a box of fish fingers fell out, you lost your temper and accused her of stealing Godfrey."

"It wasn't fish—"

"I said don't interrupt, Coral."

Miss Mirk dunked her biscuit into her tea and sucked the end of it, noisily, the finch tapping at her head.

"You also told Miss Mirk that if she had kidnapped God and he had come to any harm, she would live to regret it."

I gasped. Those weren't my words!

Miss Mirk's eyes slid over to meet mine. There was something in the way they glittered that kept me quiet. This was a warning; I was to leave her alone or else she'd tell Mum and Dad the truth about Gran.

Dad raked at his beard. "Coral, your behaviour today has been completely unacceptable. No matter how upset you are over something, you don't threaten people, do I make myself clear?"

It felt awful that Dad had taken Miss Mirk's side. *He hates you. Just wait until he finds out what you did. He'll never want anything to do with you again.*

My thoughts hurt worse than punches and my eyes watered.

"Is there anything you want to say to Miss Mirk?" asked Mum.

You give me the creeps and I know you've kidnapped God and I hate that you always speak so quietly and I want to wipe that smile off your face right this second.

I cleared my throat. "Miss Mirk, I'm sorry I was looking through your letter box and it was rude of me not to help you with your shopping trolley. I shouldn't have accused you of stealing God..."

"Again," Miss Mirk butted in.

"I shouldn't have accused you of stealing God – again. I hope you can forgive me," I mumbled. My body prickled as though thorns flowed through my veins.

Miss Mirk drained the last of her tea and wriggled to the edge of the sofa, so her feet could touch the ground. "I would strongly advise you to keep away from my property. If something else should happen, I will be straight over to tell your mother and father *everything*."

My head hung in shame.

Miss Mirk stood, crumbs falling from her *Antique Walnut* skirt on to the carpet.

"I'll show you out," said Mum, getting up.

Dad waited until he heard the front door close.

"I actually don't know where to start," he said. "We allowed you to do the posters on your own because we trusted you. Your mum told you to be polite to Miss Mirk. You know what she's like; she loves it if she's got something to complain about. We'll never hear the end of this."

Mum reappeared and perched on the arm of Dad's chair. I flipped the cushion over, wishing it was a shield, hoping his words would bounce off it before they could reach my ears.

Dad hadn't finished. "You lied to us about charging your phone, so when we tried to get hold of you, we couldn't, and then you went and disappeared without letting either of us know where you were. I've been driving around Saltbay for the past hour searching for you, and your mum went to the beach in the pouring rain."

Mum reached out to touch Dad's hand; he pulled it away. "Don't you think we have enough on our plates at the moment without all this? I'm never going to be able to trust you again."

I stared into the fireplace, which was blacker than

Dad's mood. There was no point in arguing. Me talking would just anger him more. Dad's voice faded away into a threatening rumble in the background. I wished Gran was here. If I ever got into trouble, she'd whisk me off for a stroll along the beach. And with *Wild Morello Cherry* cheeks and wind-tousled hair, we'd scoff ice cream: hers with raspberry sauce and mine with a Flake. And no matter what, I always felt better.

"Coral!" barked Dad. "Are you even listening?"

I blinked away the tears, not because of Miss Mirk knowing what I'd done or Mum and Dad's disappointment in me, but because without Gran here I didn't know how I could ever be happy again. And the thought hit me the same way a wrecking ball slams into the side of a building.

Mum came over and sat next to me. "If this had only been about Miss Mirk, we wouldn't be coming down so hard on you."

"Yes, we would," said Dad. "You don't threaten old ladies no matter how annoying they are. We've not raised you to be a thug."

"She's upset," said Mum. Her *Dew Kiss* eyeshadow caught the light and shone.

"We all are," snapped Dad.

Mum sighed, her head dipping down as she gathered her thoughts. "Your dad and I are disappointed because you lied to us. The way you behaved today means there must be a punishment, so I'm going to confiscate your phone until the end of the week."

I tried my best not to show how gutted I was.

"And you're grounded, so you can forget our trip to the cinema tonight," added Dad. "I need to take the car to the garage. I'm late as it is." He left the room, hunted through his jacket pockets for his keys, and slammed the door on his way out.

The front gate rattled as it rebounded back open.

"Your dad is missing your gran terribly and trying, in his own way, to come to terms with her loss," said Mum. "I can only guess because you're not being yourself and you were at the graveyard, you're finding it hard too?"

I thought about Gran, Miss Mirk, Lyart, Moonzy and Muckle Red, forcing everything deeper down inside me.

"Is there something you'd like to talk about?"

She fanned her fingers out, her nails gleaming with *Tantalizing Teal* varnish.

I knew Mum was only trying to be nice. Except I couldn't say a word to her, not if she was already worried about me. And Dad was right, they had enough to deal with without me adding to their woes.

"Coral?" said Mum.

"I miss Gran so much," I said. "Wish I could see her again."

"Oh, Coral." Mum's eyes thickened with tears as she leaned in to give me a hug. A feeling inside me spread to my heart, making every single part of me feel alive with certainty. The only thing that would make me happy again was talking to Gran, so I could tell her I was sorry for what I had done and that I loved her to the moon and back.

CHAPTER

8

I sat up in the dark, straining my ears to catch muffled voices from the TV in the lounge, or the dishes clattering as Dad set the table for breakfast in the morning. But there was only silence. My clock said four minutes past twelve and the house stayed quiet, as though it too had fallen asleep.

I'd been so lucky to get out alive from the graveyard earlier, it seemed foolish even to consider going back. Yet I couldn't stop thinking about what Lyart had said about Muckle Red and the harm he'd do if he was set free. The thought of him prowling the streets of Saltbay made me shudder. And then there was the matter of Gran. If I didn't show up tonight, I'd miss any chance I had of seeing her again.

I pulled on my leggings and hopped on the floor, as I tried to stick my feet into my high-tops. Lastly, I grabbed my coat, slung on my rucksack and tugged down my hat.

Sliding open the window, I eased myself on to the ledge, ignoring my grumbling heart. I was about to sneak out in the middle of the night to a graveyard, which was home to an evil entity, and on top of all of this, I'd not long been grounded by Mum and Dad. If I got caught, they would never trust me again. And if I was captured by Muckle Red, I doubted I'd live to tell the tale.

Before I could change my mind, I launched myself on to a branch and wobbled as I grasped handfuls of leaves above my head to steady myself. The branch dipped and swayed, but held strong as I walked towards the trunk. I took my time clambering down and lowered myself on to the last branch, dangling in the air until my hands started to slip. I let go, landing in a heap with a groan. I peered up at Mum and Dad's window to see if their light had clicked on – thankfully, their room stayed *Burnt Peppercorn*.

The night was cool enough to make the stars shiver. The moon was so huge I was amazed it had even risen. I strained my eyes trying to catch witches flying across its craters, but there were none, which was just as well, otherwise I would have turned tail and gone straight back to bed.

A rustling noise made me jump. A hedgehog scooted out from the shrubs and snuffled its way across the grass, following a winding path of *Looking Glass* slug trails in the moonlight.

I let my breath out and peered over at the hole in Miss Mirk's blinds. Anger fizzed around my heart at the thought God was trapped inside. I slunk across the grass to the gate, which gave a rusty scream as I opened it. I checked the alleyway was empty and squeezed myself through the narrow gap.

That's when I spied a figure heading right towards me.

I shrank behind the recycling bin, wishing I was inside it.

The footsteps ground to a halt at Miss Mirk's gate. I peeked out and saw the silhouette of a small, round figure. Miss Mirk stepped into the middle of the alleyway. I flattened myself against the bin and held my breath. After what seemed like for ever, grit crunched under her heel as she returned to her gate. It opened and clicked shut. I didn't move a muscle. Gran and I had watched too many films where the baddie sounded as though he had gone, but was only pretending, so he could catch the good guy unawares. When her door rattled, I decided it was safe to stand. If Miss Mirk had caught me outside at this time of night, she would have been straight round to tell Mum and Dad. I was going to have to make sure that never happened again.

As I tiptoed past her garden, something caught my eye. What appeared to be pieces of paper were lying scattered on the ground. I stooped to pick them up and scratched my cheek. They were all posters of missing pets. Miss Mirk must have dropped them! The tops of the corners were torn, as if they'd been ripped down from where they'd been hanging.

Why would Miss Mirk be sneaking about at night,

pinching lost pet posters? Did she not want people to know these poor creatures were missing? None of this made sense . . . unless Miss Mirk was the one who had stolen them in the first place! That would explain why she was so eager to keep me away from her home and the reason she had tins of cat food in her trolley. And if she *was* kidnapping pets, God would be inside her house, being held captive against his will.

I folded the posters and shoved them into my rucksack. I didn't have time to figure all this out now, but one thing was for certain: I was going to have to keep a much closer eye on Miss Mirk from now on and work out a way to get God back.

I swept along the street faster than a stick in a river. I'd never seen the town this empty before. I kept checking behind me but the only things moving at this hour were the changing traffic lights. I veered into what Dad and I renamed Satellite Dish Street and took the next left into Perfect Lawn Avenue. One of the windows had a gap-toothed pumpkin in it. I'd always loved Halloween, but had been scared senseless at the thought of ghosts roaming free for a day until midnight. Now I knew they roamed around all the time. I shivered and sped up.

When I reached the graveyard, I peeped over the wall. The headstones were standing in line: a silent army guarding their dead.

The terrified angel glowed *Swan Queen* under the massive moon. I checked its outstretched wings for the hint of a flap or a quiver. It was one thing walking along deserted streets by myself, but quite another going into a graveyard, alone, at this hour. If something happened, no one would hear me scream. Just as I was thinking it would be better to return in the morning, someone laughed.

I pushed the gate open, taking a few steps in. My heart thumped in my ears and I had the strangest feeling I was being watched.

Suddenly a beech nut smacked off my shoulder and I yelped. I stared in the direction it had been thrown from, but I couldn't see a soul.

"*Who's there?*" I whispered.

A movement caught my eye. Peering out from behind the ivy was a young girl, who ducked when she saw me.

My blood ran as cold as melting glacier water. If Muckle Red knew she was here, her life could be in great danger.

I hurried towards her but she was nowhere to be seen.

"Hey! Where have you gone?" I said, catching a glimpse of a *Whisper White* dress disappearing behind a tall stone cross. I bolted after her, aware I was getting further away from the gate. However, after everything Lyart had told me about the Heart Collector, she wouldn't be safe.

I passed a row of graves, which were small and leaned backwards as though they'd suffered a terrible fright.

Surrounded by trees and beech hedges, I found myself in a clearing at the end of the churchyard I hadn't been in before.

The little girl came out from behind a weeping willow.

"Do your mum and dad know you are here?" I asked softly, careful to not scare her away.

She shook her head.

I crouched. "Do you want to go home?"

The girl moved into the moonlight; her hair shone *Raven Wing.*

"My name's Coral Glen. What's yours?"

Her smile faded.

"*Muckle Red!*" she growled in a deep voice. *Lunar Eclipse Blue* veins spread across her cheeks and her hair faded to *Pearl Kingdom.* Right in front of my eyes, she disappeared, leaving behind a pile of bones in her place.

The moon tried its best to squeeze behind a cloud.

I leapt to my feet and started to run. A strong wind whipped up from nowhere. The trees thrashed and leaves flew into my eyes. I gasped as the air swirled around me, pushing me back, as though I was surrounded by an invisible wall of ice.

Without warning, bones shot up through the earth. One by one, they stacked themselves on top of each other, cracking as they clicked into place. A skull hurtled out of the ground and landed on top of the skeleton. There was a loud crunch as it swivelled in my direction.

My heart stopped when its jaw pinged open.

Flesh and cloth slithered over the skeleton. A shock of *Red Slash* hair sprouted from the skull, a patch covered its left eye and a chain with hearts strung on it dangled from the neck. With a final snap, Muckle Red sprang to life.

Fear rooted me to the spot. The graveyard became mountain-peak cold.

"W-what happened to the girl?" I blurted out.

"Once, many moons ago, she would have been warm, scabby-kneed and hair tangles, but now she's only good for foxes to chew on." He kicked at her pile of bones, sending them scattering. "I play all sorts of games with skeletons. Can be any person I wish in this dump."

My breath turned into ghosts in the air. I glanced wildly around for Lyart and Moonzy; they were the reason I'd come here and now they were nowhere to be seen. I was on my own with a wicked spirit who collected hearts as a hobby.

Icicles appeared on the weeping willow, hanging from the branches like frozen tears. The grass sparkled with frost and crackled as Muckle Red stepped towards me.

"All alone?" He twisted his head to ogle at what beat faster than wings behind my ribcage.

My teeth started to chatter.

Muckle Red smacked his *North Sea* lips together. "You should be fast asleep: instead you're in a yard of stones, worms and bone dust. Why?"

I wished I could stop swaying. "I-I don't make a habit of hanging around places like this."

Muckle Red straightened himself up.

"No? A little birdie told me a girl was in here earlier swapping words with the Keeper of Halloway. She was made from messy curls, a red coat, black-and-white legs and scuffed feet, much the same as yourself."

"Wasn't me." My insides were screaming at me to run, except if I bolted, he'd know for certain I was lying. I cursed myself for coming here.

Muckle Red grunted.

My head started to nip, the same as when you eat ice cream too fast and it gives you brain freeze. This wasn't sounding good, but how could Muckle Red prove I had been here earlier? And besides, if I did tell him I had spoken to Lyart, I could be in worse trouble.

"Oi! Skaw!" boomed Muckle Red.

I scanned the gravestones, wondering who or what was going to show up.

A large *Ashes of Roses*–coloured worm wriggled on to Muckle Red's shoulder.

"Is this the girl you saw that was all whispers and plotting with Lyart today?"

The worm squinted at me. I never knew they had teeth.

My eyes flicked to the gravestones. If I was to make a run for it, I'd need to know exactly where I was going.

"Why are you more snail than worm, Skaw?" Muckle Red's question was brittle with impatience. "Is it or is it not her?"

"Aye, it's her without a doubt," confirmed the worm.

I launched myself forward like a greyhound out of a trap and kicked Muckle Red's leg so hard, bone splintered. Muckle Red tried to grab me. I knocked his arm away and shoved him with all my might. Skaw cursed as they crashed down on the grass.

Sprinting towards the graves, I sneaked a look behind me. A pile of bones lay where Muckle Red had been standing only seconds ago. They started to burrow their way back into the earth.

Flashing past the headstones, I spotted the fearful angel and skidded on to the path, relieved to see the gate. As I charged towards it, something whistled past me faster than rockets.

An arctic-cold wind knocked me off my feet and rolled me along the ground. When I finally came to a halt, bruises blossomed on my skin.

Bones burst through the earth, knitting together, until Muckle Red appeared. He twisted his skull on, and flesh once again crept over his skeleton. The hearts swinging from his chain dripped *Ox Blood* red. It was hard to imagine they'd once belonged to children. A wave of sickness hit me. No wonder Lyart and Moonzy were so desperate to prevent him from escaping; he had to be destroyed, at all cost.

Muckle Red slapped his neck bones into place. "I never knew girls could be so lightning-filled and cornered-cat feisty."

I pushed down the terror and allowed rage to

bubble up inside me. I sprang to my feet. "I'm going to do *everything* I can to make sure you never leave here, Muckle Red!" I bent to grab a conker and hurled it at him. It struck his skull, knocking a chunk off it.

"Oi!" screeched the worm.

"Any more of that and you'll never see Lyart again." There was something in the way Muckle Red spoke that reminded me he was a killer.

Lyart and Moonzy had left me all alone with him, too scared to show their faces. "Why should I care what happens to him?" I yelled.

Muckle Red's eye glinted and the corners of his mouth twitched. "Because you need Lyart if you're to see Granny one last time."

The graveyard wobbled.

Muckle Red knows Lyart is planning on taking you to your gran on the night of the Hallow moon. You're done for now.

The cold sucked all the oxygen from the night air, making it hard to breathe. My body throbbed and my limbs felt tombstone-heavy. I wished to walk away; to go home and forget a world with Muckle

Red in it even existed. However, if I left now, I would never get the chance to talk to Gran again: the only thing that mattered to me.

I gritted my teeth so hard my temples hurt. "What have you done with Lyart?"

"He's somewhere in the graveyard, safe, provided you do as I command."

I squared up to Muckle Red. "What do you want?"

"Witch's tears, cannibal bones and a wrecker bird; all before the strike of twelve on Halloween," he said.

I gasped. They were exactly the same objects Lyart wanted to make sure Muckle Red didn't get his hands on! If I collected them, Muckle Red would be able to escape the graveyard and kill again! But if I didn't, I'd never be able to find Lyart and see Gran.

I stamped the ground with my foot. This was an utterly impossible position to be put in!

I didn't want to give up my chance to be with Gran, except there was no way I could free Muckle Red either ... unless I gathered the objects and then hid them somewhere, so I could use them to guarantee Lyart's safe release. Then all I would have to do is make sure Muckle Red never found them and he'd be destroyed for once and for all when the Hallow moon left at midnight!

I kept my face still, careful not to give away that I'd hatched a plan. "I don't even know what a wrecker bird is."

"The clock is ticking, Coral Glen." Muckle Red tossed Skaw over to me.

"What are you playing at, Muckle Red?" spat the worm.

I gripped Skaw carefully by the scruff of his neck so he couldn't bite me.

"Help her bring the things I need, and you can escape this earth prison with me to experience the wonders of the world."

"Really? You'd take me with you? As your travel companion?"

"Don't let me down, worm, and keep a watchful eye on her," barked Muckle Red.

Although I wasn't happy being stuck with Skaw, he might be of some use. Perhaps, being a worm, he'd know what a wrecker bird was. I shoved him into my pocket and closed the flap to silence his cursing.

"One last thing, Coral Glen: trick me and it'll be the last thing you ever do." Muckle Red vanished, leaving a trail of bones scattered across the grass.

The trees trembled, sending a flurry of leaves to the ground.

My heart plummeted into the depths of my stomach. I only had four nights to gather witch's tears, cannibal bones and a wrecker bird for Lyart, and if they fell into Muckle Red's hands, I'd release an evil spirit back into the town and I'd never see Gran again. How was I supposed to do all this when I'd been grounded by my parents and I was stuck with a useless worm for company?

One thing was for certain: I was going to need all the help I could get. Muckle Red had mentioned Lyart but not Moonzy. Had she managed to escape from him? I wasn't sure I could trust Skaw, but the gargoyle would be as eager to find Lyart as I was.

I took a deep breath and walked towards the crooked headstone.

*

I crept along the passageway, halting every time I heard a noise. The glamps shone *Deep Sea Dive* blue, all except for one, which glowed brighter than the sun and then flashed *Breath of Spring*, something I'd not seen a glamp do before. I stopped, watching as it whirled faster. The strongest urge to smash it came over me. I'd give anything not to have a care in the world again – except I'd urgent matters to deal with.

What had Muckle Red done with Lyart? I hoped he was OK and that he hadn't been harmed. I bolted along the corridor to his room, checking above the doorway, but Moonzy wasn't there.

The door to the chamber was hanging off its hinges. All the coffins had been smashed, bones were scattered everywhere and there was a giant pile of splintered wood where his desk had been.

I pulled Skaw out from my pocket.

"Muckle Red did this, didn't he? What has he done with the gargoyle?"

Skaw avoided my eyes. Being saddled with a nasty worm was perhaps going to be more trouble than it was worth. I rifled through my rucksack for the tear catcher and shoved him inside it.

I knelt and searched for Moonzy under the rubble. I found a rusty key and a horseshoe but not the gargoyle. As I neared the bottom of a pile, my fingernails scraped against something rougher than a nail file. It was half of a large *Fire Brick* wing! I dug deeper, looking for other fragments of stone until, finally, I found a part of her face.

"Moonzy! Are you OK?"

Her eyes fluttered. "Lyart?" she croaked.

"Muckle Red's hidden him and won't tell me where he is until I find the objects he needs to break the spell. You said you can leave the graveyard; will you help me? It's the only way we can get Lyart back."

"I'll do anything. *Anything*," Moonzy said without hesitation, before spluttering grit from her lips.

"Are you in pain?" I asked, pressing my hand to her forehead.

"I can fix myself, when I'm little less tired."

I glanced at all the pieces of broken stone. They'd be too heavy for me to carry at the one time.

"Coral," Moonzy croaked. "I don't need them any more."

"I could return for the rest of you?"

"It's time for a change," said Moonzy, managing a weak smile.

I could tell she was exhausted and I didn't want to bother her with any more questions. I wrapped her face up gently in my scarf and placed her inside my rucksack. Skaw bashed himself against the glass of the tear catcher as he writhed around. I tucked him into my pocket.

I left the chamber, hurrying along the corridor. Every now and again I paused, certain I could hear something in the tunnels behind me.

CHAPTER
9

Mum burst into my room, throwing the curtains open. The sunshine stretched in to wake up each and every one of the colours on my walls. I yawned, happy to see them. And then, as sure as *Dark Granite* clouds bring rain, I remembered Gran wasn't with us any more. Muckle Red's words came back to me and the familiar feeling of heaviness returned to weigh me down. It was a wonder I didn't sink into the mattress and disappear.

"What have you been doing?" Mum frowned at the carpet.

I sat up and winced, sore from last night. That was when I realized I was still wearing my clothes. I'd been so exhausted after dragging myself in through the window, I'd crawled straight into bed without changing.

Before Mum could notice, I covered myself up with the duvet. I didn't want to have to do a whole lot of explaining about something I wouldn't even know where to begin with.

"Is that mud?" Mum inspected the carpet closer.

"I was out . . . in the garden."

Mum continued to stare at me in a way that indicated the conversation was far from over.

"Searching for God. Must have got it on my shoes checking the flower beds. Sorry."

"How many times have I told you to. . ." Mum fell silent. I followed her wide-eyed stare. There, beside my desk, was a large *Ashes of Roses* worm.

Skaw had escaped from the tear catcher!

Mum threw the window open. A breeze raced in, and the paint charts did a Mexican wave around the room.

She picked up Skaw, gingerly, between her thumb and forefinger.

This woke me up quicker than a bucket of ice being tipped over my head. If Skaw vanished, so would my chances of rescuing Lyart and seeing Gran.

"Mum!" I yelled, just as she chucked the worm towards the window.

Skaw flew through the air, hit the curtain and dropped to the floor.

"Look what you've made me do!" Mum jogged fast on the spot, flapping her arms, the way people do when they're squeamish about something they've just touched.

"Don't throw him . . . I mean *it*, out the window!" I squawked.

"Why not!" Mum shouted.

"Because it's Isla's," I said, surprising myself with the lie.

"What is Isla doing with a worm? She'd pass out if a greenfly landed on her."

"The worm is for a school project and Isla said she'd keep it – only their spaniel tried to eat the thing, so I said I'd take it." I studied every movement on Mum's face to see if she believed me or not.

"Where were you keeping it?" she asked.

"In a jar. With earth. And compost, so it doesn't starve."

"You never said." Her puzzled expression vanished. "Of course, you haven't had a chance what with everything. . ." Her words trailed off and she perched on the edge of the bed. I made sure my shoes were tucked under the covers.

"How are you feeling?" she asked.

"Tired," I said, relieved I could finally speak the truth.

"You've dark circles under your eyes." Mum smoothed the duvet with her hand.

"Thanks."

Mum had straightened her hair. Although you'd swear it was *Pain au Chocolat*, when it caught the light it glowed *Ravishing Red*, as if the sun had just performed a magic trick. Her skin shimmered, reminding me of the inside of a shell. I'd tried putting make-up on once, but Gran had told me I resembled a *lady of the night*. I took this to mean someone who worked in the twenty-four-hour garage. Gran always said my eyes were the same as the ocean because all the greens, blues and greys constantly changed depending on the light and there was nothing cosmetics could do to make them any prettier than they already were.

My ribcage shrank and it was painful for my heart to beat. "Are you off out?" I asked, pushing my thoughts to the back of my mind.

Mum leaned forward and pulled a dried leaf from my hair.

"I've decided to return to work – is that OK with you?" Her *Pink Panther* lipstick and *Periwinkle Dream* eyeshadow couldn't mask the paleness of her skin or cover up the sadness in her eyes. Mum knew too, if you concentrated hard on something else, you could escape from the pain of losing Gran, for a short while.

"Your dad will be here," she said.

"Dad?"

"He's working from home." Mum put the leaf into the wastepaper basket and then prodded me. "If you can behave for the next few days – and stay well out the way of Miss Mirk – I'm sure he'll ease up on you."

How could I be on my best behaviour? I had to find a whole bunch of weird objects, release Lyart, keep an evil entity from escaping Halloway graveyard and tell Gran I loved her one last time. And avoiding Miss Mirk, after she'd kidnapped God, wasn't on the agenda either.

I sighed, except not for the reason Mum thought I was.

She leaned forward to give me a kiss, and then used her thumb to wipe the lipstick off my cheek. "Coral?"

I raised my eyebrows at her.

"Do you think the worm will be OK? It hit the carpet quite hard."

"They're tougher than you'd imagine."

"Just as well. I wouldn't be any good at giving it CPR." Mum wrinkled her nose up as she got off the bed and walked out the room. Seconds later, her head reappeared around the side of the door. "Don't forget to clean the carpet," she added.

As the noise of her heels clattering on the stairs grew faint, I threw back the covers and leapt out of bed.

Skaw was nowhere to be seen.

I got down on my hands and knees and searched all over the floor. I checked under my desk, inside my trainers and behind two sketch pads. I moved Tatty, my old stuffed squirrel, to one side and found a hair tie, before lifting up a corner of the beanbag.

"What is it with everyone thinking it's OK to hurl me about left, right, and centre? I'm no' a plastic toy out of a cracker," bellowed Skaw from the shadows.

"You were the one trying to escape." He was cool to the touch and squirmed in my fingers. The top of his head was a much darker pink than his tail and each segment of his body shone, as though Mum had lacquered him in clear nail polish. His *Slate in the Rain* eyes met mine.

"I'm *starving*." Skaw stuck his tongue out. "Your trainers taste pure disgusting, by the way." He smacked his lips. "Where's the jar you were havering on about?"

"You can have all the earth and compost you want as soon as you help us find witch's tears, cannibal bones and a wrecker bird."

He scowled, pulling the corner of his top lip up.

I opened the wardrobe, grabbed my rucksack and lifted out Moonzy's head, carefully placing it on my duvet.

She lay silent with her eyes shut.

"Moonzy?" I waited for her to stir.

The worm wriggled to the edge of the desk.

I knelt down by the side of the bed. "Hey, sleepy! Time to wake up."

Skaw tutted. "Have you completely lost it? You're talking to a lump of stone."

"Any idea how you wake up a gargoyle?" I asked, not holding my breath for an answer.

Something tapped me on the leg and I glanced down.

There, looking up at me, was Tatty, my toy squirrel. It raised its tufty ears and twitched its nose. Two crooked *Almost Oyster* felt teeth poked out from its mouth.

"I've just had the sleep of the dead – I'm a new me." The squirrel flicked its bushy tail.

My jaw dropped open.

The squirrel twitched its plastic nose. "I feel a million times lighter now. Watch this!" The stuffed toy raced over the floor, leapt from the radiator on to the top of the wardrobe before jumping off and landing on the beanbag, where it rolled over on its front, propping its head up with its paws. "I love how colourful your room is. My eyeballs are going to pop with happiness."

A noise I'd never heard myself make before escaped from my lips.

The squirrel tilted its head to the side. "Oh! Sorry. Should have said. I'm not a real squirrel – it's me! Moonzy!"

Skaw peered at the stuffed toy, who scratched its belly before shaking itself.

"This place is a total madhouse," muttered the worm.

The squirrel swivelled its head to see who had just spoken. It was the first time I'd ever heard Tatty growl. The *Autumn Russet* fur on the back of its neck stood on end as the toy bounced on to the desk, pinning the worm down. Skaw's colour changed from *Ashes of Rose* to *Vigorous Violet*.

"Where is he?" squeaked the squirrel. "What have you done with Lyart?"

It really was Moonzy! I hurried over to the desk,

where it took me three goes to separate them.

"What did you do that for?" Moonzy glowered at me.

Skaw spluttered, his sides heaving as he gasped for breath.

"Killing the worm isn't going to do any good," I pointed out.

"It'd make me feel a whole lot better," Moonzy snarled.

"Who is *this*?" Skaw sat up straight as periscopes, wary.

"Skaw, this is Moonzy, a friend of Lyart's."

"What is that *worm* doing here?" The squirrel threw a glance at Skaw that was dirtier than a mudslide.

"Skaw is going to help us," I replied.

Moonzy snorted. "You mean spy on us."

I sat on the bed, pointing at the gargoyle's head. "I think you've got some explaining of your own to do. One minute you're a lump of stone and the next you're Tatty, my favourite childhood toy."

Moonzy hopped down from the desk, thudding on the carpet. With a shake of her tail she bounded up on to the bed beside me. When she spoke, she wasn't even out of breath. "I'm a poltergeist."

"What is that?" I furrowed my brow.

"I'm a ghost that can inhabit different objects, which means I can be anything I please."

"Is this why you can leave the graveyard but the other ghosts can't?"

"Exactly, Coral!" grinned the squirrel. "But as I mentioned before, I've not left Halloway in for ever and I'm frightened that what lies beyond the walls will bamboozle me. However, I'll be fine with you there."

"Who are you kidding? You only change into different things because your real face would make onions cry," muttered Skaw out the corner of his mouth.

"At least I'll never be stuck in a useless body such as yours, Skaw," she fired back.

Skaw whacked a pen with his tail. It shot like an arrow towards Moonzy, who ducked as it whizzed past her. "Being a poltergeist means I can read auras too," she said, sticking her nose in the air and ignoring the worm.

"What are those?" I put the pen on my bedside

table, in case Moonzy decided to launch it at Skaw.

"It's the energy field around the body, and you can tell a lot about someone depending on what colour it is. Lyart's aura is the best: it's the purest form of bright green, which means he's kind and loves people, animals and nature. Worm-head's over there isn't so good – it's black and muddy pink, so he's fearful, guarded and dishonest. No surprises there, then."

The worm shook his head. "You're talking out of your—"

"Skaw!" I chided.

"Coral, you have a grey aura and this means you're sad because you're grieving."

I swallowed hard, determined to stop my eyes from filling up. "Whether we like it or not, we're all going to have to work together and figure out how to get witch's tears, cannibal bones and a wrecker bird. And right now, thanks to a school trip, the only thing I know is there might be a witch buried under a boulder on Guiltree Hill. And if it's true, the stone is so enormous, I doubt even Superman could shift it, let alone us. Any thoughts?"

"I sneeze whenever there's a witch nearby." Moonzy cleaned her nylon whiskers with her paws. "It might help us find another one in a café or an amusement arcade."

"Thank you, Moonzy. Skaw? Anything?"

Skaw's *Slate in the Rain* eyes darkened. "It's against my better judgement to collaborate with a vile squirrel and a girl whose room looks as if there's been an explosion in a paint factory." Skaw flushed the entire length of his body. "However, I want the spell imprisoning Muckle Red to be broken."

Moonzy's ears fell back as though his words were difficult to hear.

The worm stared out of the window at the cauliflower-shaped clouds lit *Imperial White* by the sun. "Muckle Red's been desperate to leave Halloway for ages. He'll be much happier when he's away from the graveyard; it'll be better for his health."

"Better for his health maybe, but not anyone else's. He's a murderous, coffin-dodging, crooked sack of bones and he makes me sick!" Moonzy's eyes flashed and her tail stiffened.

Skaw whipped his head round at her. "You don't

have a clue what you're talking about. He's no' into any of that nonsense any more; he's a reformed character. He wouldn't harm a fly these days!"

Moonzy laughed, clutching her belly. "That's the funniest thing I've heard. He's got you fooled good and proper."

"Ach, away and boil your head," snapped Skaw. "Just so we're clear – I will lend a hand, but only because it means Muckle Red and I can leave Halloway."

"OK, you two; enough. We don't have to get on, we just need to figure this out, together," I said.

Moonzy scampered on to the chair, using her tail to keep her balance. "You're right, Coral. Time is not on our side – there are only three nights until the Hallow moon and the question is: where do witches, cannibals and wrecker birds hang out? I always ask Lyart when I don't know something. Who do you ask, Coral?"

"Google," I said with a shrug.

"Who's she?" Moonzy blinked.

"A search engine on the computer my dad is working on today."

The squirrel didn't move one muscle. Not even an ear twitched.

Skaw wriggled away from the sunlight on the desk, twisting in *Ashes of Roses* and *Drizzling Mist* spirals. "You two are as much use as a tyrannosaurus rex with no teeth. Everyone knows there's only one person in Saltbay who will have all the answers."

"Don't tell me – a wise old goblin who lives in an enchanted dell in a drainage pipe under the motorway?"

"No," said Skaw, frowning at me. "A librarian."

"Of course! Mrs Shellycoat – she's a friend of my gran's." I paused. "She *was* a friend of my gran's." My bottom lip trembled.

Moonzy scampered on to the bed, her ears swivelling out to the sides. "Don't worry, Coral, we'll track everything down so we can rescue Lyart and you can be with your gran again." The squirrel patted my hand. "My mum used to tell me if you picture something really good happening in your head, it makes it come true."

The worm raised his eyes as if he was concentrating hard. "I'm visualizing you under the wheels of a bus."

"*Skaw!*" I warned.

Moonzy carried on. "Even if you don't believe me, thinking about something good makes you feel much better than thinking about something bad, and that's a fact."

If I was ever upset or afraid when I was younger, I would cuddle the squirrel, and now here it was comforting me, for real. I smiled at Moonzy and then my face fell. "I've been grounded."

Skaw gave such a deep sigh the Post-it note stuck on the lamp fluttered.

Moonzy sprung on to the floor, pacing back and forth, deep in thought. Just as I was going to ask her if she had a plan, there was a knock at the door.

I leapt into bed, covering myself with the duvet. Skaw recoiled and Moonzy flopped over on her side.

"Are you awake?" said a muffled voice through the door.

"Yes," I replied.

Dad appeared carrying a mug of tea and a plate of toast smothered in lemon curd, which was my favourite. He plonked the tea on the bedside table. It sloshed over the side of the mug and as he bent to put the plate down, the toast slipped off it. I managed to catch it before it landed on the covers.

"It is fortunate I'm not a waiter, otherwise we'd be destitute." Dad patted the top of his head, checking his hair wasn't sticking up.

"What does that mean?" I took a bite of the toast, which tasted all buttery and zingy with lemon.

"It means we wouldn't have a penny to our name. Your mum was telling me we have a house guest."

I nodded, taking another huge bite of toast.

Dad spotted Skaw on the desk. "Oh, he's an impressive fellow." Dad scratched his beard. "I didn't know worms had eyes?"

"He's a rare breed from ... Perth."

Dad gave me a sideways glance. I thought it might be a good idea to change the subject. "Has anyone been in touch about God?"

He picked some fluff off his shirt and stuck his hands in his pockets. "I went on to the site earlier; there have been quite a few shares of his picture."

I swallowed the last of the toast and sipped at the tea. Dad tapped the side of his mouth with his finger. Patting around my lips, I found the blob of lemon curd. I wiped it off, only to make my fingers stickier than superglue. "Sorry about yesterday," I said, rubbing my hands together. The last thing I needed right now was to fall out with Mum and Dad.

"I'm not saying what you did is OK – we're all off kilter at the moment, so thanks for the apology. However, don't think for a minute I'm letting you off the hook. You broke my trust, Coral."

"Do you know anything about witches in Saltbay?" I asked.

"Coral, if this is a ploy to let you go out on Halloween, it's not going to work." Dad sounded exhausted, even though the day had barely begun.

I had another thought. "I know I'm grounded but I really need to return a book to the library because it's overdue and I don't want to upset Mrs Shellycoat, especially when she's been so kind."

Dad walked towards the window, unaware Moonzy was right in his path.

I held my breath.

Dad stepped over her.

I let it out, relieved.

He still hadn't said no, so I decided to carry on. "I'd go straight there and once I've chosen another book, come right back. I'll ask if Mrs Shellycoat could put up a poster of God on the library noticeboard too."

Dad's jaw wiggled, a sure sign he was mulling something over he was in two minds about. He closed the window, crossed the room and trod on Moonzy, who squeaked. He halted to see what had made the noise.

"Is that Tatty?" he asked, picking the squirrel up. He poked the squirrel's stomach hard with his finger and it squeaked again, this time sounding much higher-pitched.

"Dad! Careful not to break it."

"I thought your mum had carted this off to the charity shop?"

"I fished it out the bag."

Dad's face lit up. "Your gran made this and every night we had to put it by the door to guard you, otherwise you refused to go to sleep. One time, Gran took you on a trip to the fair at Girvenhall and you left Tatty on the bus. You were inconsolable and kept the entire household up all night with your wails, so your gran drove to the bus depot the next day where, luckily, someone had handed Tatty in. And we were all ecstatic because it meant we could get a proper night's sleep again." Dad handed me the toy, his smile fading.

Moonzy glared at me.

Dad rubbed his eyes, turning the whites of them *In the Pink*. "If Gran was here, she'd be cross with me for not letting you go. I know how important books were to her and how much she loved taking you there. Come home immediately, Coral. Don't let me down this time."

"I won't." I pulled back the covers and hurried over to the wardrobe before remembering I was still in my clothes.

Dad collected up my mug and plate. "Did you have your shoes on in bed?"

"Yes," I said, trying to sound as though it was no big deal.

"I thought you were supposed to do crazy stuff when you were a teenager?" Dad balanced the mug on top of the plate.

"I'll be one soon." I shrugged.

"Oh, well then, that explains everything." The cup rattled as Dad closed the door behind him.

CHAPTER
10

The library was five minutes away on Cough Street.
Dad and I had named it this because the traffic
lights were constantly at *Ruby Starlet*, the road
snarled with cars and the air clogged with choking
fumes.

The flap on my coat pocket rose and Moonzy
popped her head out. I'd tucked Skaw into my scarf
where I could keep a close eye on him. But he'd
been warned if there was any nonsense, he'd be put
straight back into the tear catcher and there would
be no compost for dinner.

I hurried along Our Street, only stopping to check God's poster.

"What happened to the other half of its tail?" asked Skaw, spitting stray hairs of scarf wool from his mouth.

I checked we were alone before I spoke. "We think he got into a fight with a fox. This is my gran's cat, God, and he's missing." I ran my hand over the poster. Yesterday's rain had wrinkled God's face and his *Midnight Oasis* black coat bled *Purple Grape* at the edges. "Except I'm pretty sure I know where he is," I said more to myself than to Moonzy or Skaw. I continued on down the road. Dad had allowed me to go to the library and I wanted to be quick, so he knew he could trust me again.

Moonzy gasped at everything. I suppose if you'd spent years stuck in a dark tunnel, this would be a riot of new sights, scents, sounds and colours. Skaw smacked his lips hungrily every time we passed a patch of earth.

I sped down Weed Lane and cut through Dumpers' Paradise on to Cough Street. After crossing the road, I stood outside Saltbay Library.

Its *Desert Fawn* sandstone walls had dark patches on them as if each block of stone had been dipped into soot. Everything from the smooth-as-sea-pebble steps to the brass name plate with the fingerprints on it was as familiar to me as my own home, except today it felt different. This was the first time I'd been here without Gran and even though the place was full of books, it was packed with memories too.

I leaned back, pulling the door open. It greeted me with a low whine and then a squeak as it closed behind me.

Long lines of sunlight broke in through the windows, shining spotlights on the sparkling dust that danced in the air. The smell of pages, book spines and shiny covers filled my nose. I could hear the rustle of newspapers being turned, the rattle-tap of computer keys and someone coughing. Gran always said a library wouldn't be a library if it didn't have people hacking or sneezing in it.

I walked over the *Nectar of the Goddess, Candied Pumpkin* and *Slice of Heaven*–coloured carpet. The pattern on it was so bold, I lifted my feet in case I tripped over the shapes.

Mrs Shellycoat's face brightened. Her spectacles always slipped down her nose when she spoke, but they never fell off. She plonked a pile of books on the reception desk. "Hello, dear."

I concentrated on not glancing over at the leather chairs where Gran and I always sat when we were reading. They were as soft as marshmallows and air would whoosh out of them if you threw yourself down on one, which always made Gran and me snort.

Swallowing hard, I blinked away the memory and fished the book out from my rucksack. "I'm sorry, Mrs Shellycoat, it's late."

Mrs Shellycoat took it from me. Her nails were painted *Tangerine Grove* and she had a diamond ring on her finger. Sometimes, if it caught the light, you could see every single colour that existed in the world in it.

"Coral, after what you and your mum and dad are going through, it's a wonder you remembered you'd borrowed the book in the first place." She paused. "I noticed a poster on my way in this morning. Have you found God?"

My throat narrowed and I could feel tears one-more-sad-thought away from my eyes. The fact I said nothing told her everything.

"Do you have any going spare?" she asked.

I pulled one from my rucksack and gave it to her. Mrs Shellycoat smoothed it down flat on her desk to examine it.

"Oh my! He is a big fellow, isn't he? That'll stand in his favour as he'll be all the easier to spot. If it's OK with you, I'll put this on our noticeboard?"

"Thank you, Mrs Shellycoat. I found some others abandoned on the street; would it be all right to put them up too?"

"Of course," said Mrs Shellycoat. "I'll show them to Morven Horseshire, the vet. She's always in here." Mrs Shellycoat leaned in and lowered her voice. "She has a liking for adventure stories full of danger, brooding heroes and unbridled passion."

I wasn't too sure what she meant. We'd taken God in to Morvern Horseshire's clinic once. Her hair was curlier than mine and she was quieter than a sleeping cat.

Mrs Shellycoat straightened back up. "Loads

of people will see it because the place is going like a county fair today. We've got a class of Primary Threes meeting an author. You wouldn't believe the racket such tiny lungs can make."

"Mrs Shellycoat, I was wondering if I could ask you for help ... with my school project?"

Her face lit up as if she'd just been told she'd won a prize. "Of course, Coral."

"I'm wanting to know if there are any books on ... on..."

Moonzy prodded me from inside my pocket, making me twist awkwardly to the side.

"OnwitchescannibalsandwreckerbirdsinSaltbay?" I said it so fast it came out as one word.

Mrs Shellycoat didn't bat an eyelid. "The projects you young ones work on are so wildly exciting compared to what we had to do in my day. Everything we have about witches usually flies off the shelves at this time of year with Halloween coming up. Did I hear you right? Did you say cannibals and wrecker birds?"

My blush matched the same shade of *Vermillion Party* as her jumper. Mrs Shellycoat pushed her glasses up her nose. "I'll let you into a secret: inside every person is a reader just waiting to find the right book. You must always read what you're interested in and not what others think you should be reading. I'll need to do a search and fortunately I relish a good challenge; it keeps me youthful. Take a look in the nature section, which is halfway along the second aisle to the right. There may be information on wrecker birds there. I'll come and find you when I have some suggestions." Mrs Shellycoat's glasses slid to the very tip of her nose.

I grinned at her, showing my teeth, because she hadn't mentioned Gran and this made my first time back in the library a tiny bit easier.

"Coral?" Miss Shellycoat gazed at me.

"Uh-huh?"

"There is a worm on your shoulder."

Skaw blinked at us both.

"Are worms not allowed in here?" I asked, cupping my hand over Skaw, who squirmed underneath my fingers.

Her mouth twitched. "Only bookworms."

"Thank you, Mrs Shellycoat." I sped off towards

the shelves she'd pointed to and shot down the aisle. Away from prying eyes, I flattened myself against a wall of novels. The shelf shook and three hardbacks tumbled to the ground, their pages flapping.

"What are you doing drawing attention to yourself?" I hissed through my teeth.

"I agreed I'd help you find the objects, but that's it. I don't answer to you and can do exactly as I please."

"I vote we feed him to the next pigeon." Moonzy's head poked out from my pocket.

"Enough!" I said, stamping my foot, which sent a further two books crashing to the floor. I plucked Skaw off my shoulder. "If we don't stop bickering amongst ourselves, Moonzy won't have a hope of rescuing Lyart, I'll never see my gran again and you won't be able to travel across the world with your pal."

Just at that moment a small boy zoomed around the corner, making the vrooming noises of a car engine. Moonzy ducked out of sight.

The boy squealed to a halt as soon as he spotted the worm dangling in front of him.

Skaw glowered at the child. "What you staring at, snot nose?"

The boy's face scrunched up as he wailed louder than an ambulance. I whipped Skaw behind my back.

A woman in a *Lost Blue* and *Snow White* polka dot dress appeared.

"That worm spoke to me," said the boy, pointing in my direction.

"Patrick Logan! We *never* call girls names or we end up in trouble," scolded the lady.

The boy started to cry again, forcing a fresh trail of thick *Pistachio Haze* gunk out of his nose. The lady gave me an apologetic glance and led him away at arm's length.

When the coast was clear, I fixed Skaw with a stare that could have withered freshly picked flowers. "If I didn't know any better, I'd say you were deliberately trying to cause trouble."

Moonzy piped up, "We don't need him, Coral. He's bad news."

Skaw's eyes darkened. "I'm here because you two couldn't figure your way out of a one-way street with signposts."

"We only have three days to find the objects and the pair of you are more interested in arguing the whole time. Why are we even bothering?" My shoulders drooped as the energy drained from me the way water does from a bath that's just had the plug pulled. My head ached and my thoughts scrambled. I bent to scoop up the pile of books on the floor. As I returned them to the shelf, two small *Time-Worn Stone* eyes peered at me through the gap.

I dropped the books, wincing as my foot broke their fall.

"Wherever I go, there you are, and I ask myself if it is a coincidence or if you are following me?" It was hard to hear Miss Mirk over the sound of chattering children. She had a fox stole draped over her shoulder. It had always upset Gran if she saw Miss Mirk wearing furs. She used to say: *It takes up to forty dumb animals to make a coat, but only one to wear it*. The fox's glass eyes pleaded with me.

I shifted from one leg to the other, the bones in my foot throbbing.

"Stay away, Coral Glen, otherwise I won't be held responsible for my actions. This is your very last warning." And with that, Miss Mirk and fox vanished.

What *actions* was she talking about? Telling Mum and Dad what I'd done? Or was she meaning she'd harm God?

I gripped the bookcase to steady myself.

"Who was *that*?" asked Moonzy.

"My neighbour: Miss Mirk."

The radiator-hot air thickened, making it hard to breathe. I stumbled towards a seat at the end of the aisle. It was wooden and uncomfortable, reminding me of the pew in the church.

I stared over at Gran's favourite chair, where she would keep one eye on what she was reading and the other on the comings and goings of the library. The first day she had brought me here, she took me around as though we were in a museum full of priceless treasures. I remember Gran had beamed, just as proud of introducing me to the people she knew as she was of showing me the books.

"Coral," she had said. "Saltbay Library is better than any airport because all these books will transport you to anywhere you want to go in the world and places far beyond for free. Plus, the people-watching is way better here because nobody is in so much of a rush."

The heavy ache in my chest ground the already broken pieces of my heart into *Cut Ruby* dust. Warm tears raced each other over my cheeks.

It's your fault Gran is dead. You don't deserve to see her again. You might as well give up now because you're useless.

I buried my face in my hands.

Moonzy crawled on to my lap and reached up to squeeze my fingers with a velvety paw. "Coral, please don't stop fighting for the chance to be with your gran again. Often when things seem impossible, something miraculous will happen and it's as if the whole universe is listening to your thoughts and sending you help, just when you need it the most."

Skaw pulled a face. "What a pile of—"

"There you are, Coral. I've found something that might be of interest to you." Mrs Shellycoat ignored the stuffed squirrel on my lap and the scowling worm on my shoulder.

I dabbed at my eyes with my coat sleeves.

Mrs Shellycoat knelt beside me, her knees cracking like whips. She fished a clean tissue from her pocket and handed it to me.

I blew my nose.

She removed her glasses and polished the lenses on her jumper. "One day you'll realize the memories making you sad right now will be the very same ones you'll hold dear to your heart when you're older and this place – if it's not closed due to council cuts – will become precious to you."

I sniffed, trying not to picture Gran again in my mind, because paper and water weren't a good combination.

Mrs Shellycoat handed me the kind of book you'd expect to blow dust off before you opened it. The cover was *Lost Valley* green and its pages mottled and wrinkled as though they'd been accidentally splashed with tea. *The Folklore of Saltbay* was written in squiggly lettering in the same colour as *Pharaoh's Gold*.

"It was donated to the library by the Saltbay Historical Society. There's a section on witches and what's interesting is, all the stories are local."

Mrs Shellycoat put her glasses on and grimaced as though crouching wasn't comfortable. "I do remember reading about a series of deaths in Saltbay, back in the early eighteenth century. It was said to be the work of witches and many people were rounded up and tried for it, which won't have ended well for them."

That must have been what Lyart was talking about, except he said it was Muckle Red and not the witches at all!

Mrs Shellycoat tutted. "There were some dark times in Saltbay. If you healed the sick with herbs from the forest, it could be enough for people to brand you a witch."

I licked the salt from my lips.

"I can't let you take the book home; it's for reference only. Fortunately, or unfortunately, depending on how you look at it, any information on cannibals has drawn a blank. I'll away and see if I can find anything on the bird," said Mrs Shellycoat, getting to her feet with a groan.

"You've been brilliant, Mrs Shellycoat." I held up her tissue.

"Oh, you can keep it, it's on the house." She smiled and then rolled her eyes at the growing squeals of excited children. "I think the author has arrived." Mrs Shellycoat patted the squirrel's head. "Quite the menagerie with you today, Coral."

Mrs Shellycoat didn't wait for my reply. She strode down the aisle, tidying books as she went.

Moonzy had been right; just when I thought everything seemed hopeless, Mrs Shellycoat had given me a book on witches. And if we could somehow figure out a way to get the tears, we'd only have two other objects to find for Lyart to be released and me to talk to Gran.

The book's spine grumbled as it opened and I leafed through the pages. I scanned the section on witches, my fingers tracing the lines as I read.

"You found something?" Skaw wriggled on to my shoulder.

"A horrible worm. Came from the graveyard," Moonzy said under her breath.

"Listen to this. *In 1762, Carline Deedclathes from Halloway stood trial for several murders in Saltbay. Accused of being a witch, she cursed the town, saying she would reap revenge for the deaths of her sisters, who were burned at the stake. As punishment, she was buried alive on Guiltree Hill and a giant boulder placed over the grave to prevent her from escaping. It was recorded there were no more killings in Saltbay after this time."*

Both of Moonzy's ears flattened and she threw Skaw a look sharper than razors. "Can't believe Carline Deedclathes took the blame for those deaths." She hopped over from the arm of the chair on to a shelf.

"Muckle Red's no' proud of his past, but he's worked hard to change his character – you couldn't find a more thoughtful person or gentle soul."

Moonzy's face wrinkled up in disgust. "So how come he still wears his victims' hearts on a chain?"

"They serve as a reminder of his past wrongdoings and are the burden he must carry with him wherever he goes." Skaw wriggled off my shoulder, plopped on to my lap and slid to the floor. "Muckle Red wouldn't so much as glance in the direction of another child – end of."

I recalled Muckle Red ogling me in the graveyard. There was no way he was as trustworthy as Skaw was making out. I raised my voice to put a stop to their arguing. "We now have evidence Carline Deedclathes is buried on the hill. Thing is, we need her tears, and dead witches don't cry, so how do we bring one back to life?"

"I'm guessing it'll take some kind of magic spell." Moonzy shrugged. "I'll see if I can find something on wrecker birds." She scampered down the middle row of books, reading each title out loud as she went.

"Skaw?" I moved my foot to let him past.

"No' my area of expertise. However, I will tell you this for nothing: if you bring back something which has no' had a pulse for hundreds of years, you have to return it to the grave, otherwise you'll take its place. It's the law of nature. I'll check if there's anything on wrecker birds on the bottom shelf." Skaw wriggled towards the books.

I stared after him, stunned. Not only did we have to bring Carline Deedclathes to life, but we'd have to bury her again too, otherwise one of us would end up taking her place instead. I shivered at the thought.

Mrs Shellycoat reappeared at the end of the aisle, waving at me.

Maybe she'd found something on the wrecker bird?

I placed *The Folklore of Saltbay* on the arm of the chair and hurried towards her. Moonzy swooshed her tail and Skaw removed some carpet fluff that'd stuck to his head.

"You have a visitor, Coral." Mrs Shellycoat guided me towards the reception, where I spotted a tall figure scratching his beard.

I hesitated, wondering if I would be in even bigger trouble with Dad. I'd lost all track of time and had no idea how long we'd been here for. If more than an hour had passed by, he'd never trust me again.

I braced myself for the full force of his anger.

He stepped forward and hugged me tightly. I closed my eyes and leaned into him.

"I'm so sorry, Coral – I let you come here on your own and I should have realized it would have stirred up lots of feelings about Gran." Dad's jaw hit the top of my head softly as he spoke. His words vibrated through my skull to my heart. And just for a second, I felt at peace, but it could never have lasted.

Dad let go of me. "Next time you want to visit, I'll come too. OK? You ready to go?"

"I need to fetch a book Mrs Shellycoat gave me. Can you wait a second?"

"Actually, while Coral's doing that, could you give me a hand with these?" Mrs Shellycoat clutched the missing pet posters. The way she grinned at us, I knew it was her who had called Dad.

"I'd be happy to." Mrs Shellycoat passed him a box of drawing pins.

I hurried towards the nature section, skidding to an abrupt halt. Skaw was on the floor reading a book. Moonzy peeped down at him from the top shelf and nudged a giant encyclopedia forward with her paws. Before I could yell out a warning to Skaw, it fell down right on top of him.

I sprinted over to where the book lay, lifting it off him carefully.

Skaw lay flat out, unmoving, his skin slowly turning *Celery Sprig*, *Saffron Blush* and *Veil of Violet*.

I scooped him up in my hand, checking for cuts. "Skaw?"

"She's way more dangerous than Muckle Red," spluttered the worm.

Moonzy peered down at him with the hint of a smirk on her face.

"He's not the murderer!" I snapped at her.

"He is as good as if he helps Muckle Red out of the graveyard." The squirrel puffed up her tail.

I wrapped Skaw tightly in my tissue and tucked him into the rucksack. "Moonzy," I whispered. "I have a plan to make sure Muckle Red can't ever escape. If we gather all the objects and then hide them from him, we can force Muckle Red into telling us where Lyart is. And if they're really well hidden, there's no way Muckle Red will be able to find them before midnight."

"Which means he'll be destroyed!" chipped in Moonzy.

"Exactly! Except Skaw doesn't need to know this. We've got such little time; we need his help. So, please, do you think you can stop with the assassination attempts?"

Moonzy relaxed a little and wiggled her nose. "I didn't find anything on wrecker birds. I'm sorry."

"Thanks for searching anyway, Moonzy." I held

my coat pocket open for the squirrel. "Dad's here. We have to go."

She jumped in and I closed the flap.

Dad had finished pinning up the poster of God and the other pets, for all to see.

Without thinking, I hugged Mrs Shellycoat.

"Oh! It's like being in the grip of a boa constrictor!" She caught her glasses in time before they shot off her nose.

Dad laughed – not just a polite one; a real one.

"Thank you, Mrs Shellycoat." I handed *The Folklore of Saltbay* over to her. I really wanted to ask if she knew where I could find a spell that would bring a person back from the dead, but I thought this might be a step too far, even for her.

"I have something on the bird you were asking about, coming over from the library in Greenside. I'll drop it off for you tomorrow." Mrs Shellycoat gave us both a warning stare not to argue with her.

"Bye, Mrs Shellycoat. Thanks for keeping an eye on this one." Dad opened the door for me.

Mrs Shellycoat dipped her head slightly, before being mobbed by a shrieking group of children.

Even though Dad was holding my hand, the smile left my face by the time we'd reached the bottom of the steps because Moonzy, Skaw and I were going to have to figure out how to raise Carline Deedclathes up from her grave tonight.

CHAPTER

11

The gravel on the path up to Guiltree Hill crunched so loudly, I was sure the noise alone would be enough to wake Carline Deedclathes from the dead. It had been a miracle we hadn't disturbed Mum and Dad sneaking out of the house. Skaw and Moonzy had squabbled non-stop as I'd clambered down the tree. If Mum and Dad had cottoned on to what I was up to, they'd make it impossible for me to sneak out again, which would put an end to collecting all of the objects – something I didn't even want to think about!

Thousands of stars shimmered up above in

Heavenly White, *Pineapple Delight*, *Alice Blue* and *Orange Burst*; plane lights winked and the waves, which had been set on fire earlier by the sunset, cooled as they bathed in the *Ice Cavern* rays of the moon.

Now we were nearing the stone, the squirrel and the worm had both fallen silent.

Moonzy stared straight ahead; every now and again her nose twitched as she caught new scents. The squirrel flicked her ear a few times, as though irritated. "Funny how it's called Guiltree Hill yet there are hardly any trees on it."

We were surrounded by clumps of wilted grass and tangled patches of wild brambles, their *Provocative Plum* branches arching out like thin octopus tentacles, eager for a catch. Three trees, bullied by the wind, leaned sideways. *Black Magic*–coloured plastic bags flapped and billowed from their twisted branches, which the boys in my class had called *witches' knickers* when we'd visited here on our school trip.

The rock at the top dominated the landscape. Wide more than it was round, it sat, silent, guarding its dark secret.

All that prevented me from fleeing was the thought each step could take me closer to rescuing Lyart and being with Gran.

I buttoned my coat up, to stop the air from pinching my skin. The sea shifted and sighed far below. Even though Skaw was tucked into my beanie hat, his teeth chittered. He swung down, his nose practically touching mine. "So, what are we doing again?"

"We're going to see if there are any clues which might help us work out how to bring Carline Deedclathes back to life," I whispered, not sure why I felt the need to keep my voice down.

Skaw coughed. "That's no' much of a plan."

Moonzy scowled at him. "You got a better idea, worm-head?"

"Aye, as it happens. We go home, get some shut-eye and return to the library tomorrow. The answer will be in there, somewhere." The worm pulled himself up to sit on my hat.

"In case it has slipped your minuscule mind, we don't have the time. This needs to get sorted tonight, or your travel plans with Muckle Red will be on hold, permanently." Moonzy gave him a tight smile.

Car headlights swept round the bottom of the hill. For a moment, I wondered if it was Mum and Dad searching for me. Even if they had discovered the pile of clothes I'd shoved under my covers, they wouldn't know to look for me here. They'd check Isla's house first.

As we neared the summit, I noticed the stone was covered in swirls, drips and slashes of spray paint in *Red Riot*, *Neon Banana* and *Bubblegum*. My feet crackled over crisp packets and flattened tin cans the grass had grown over.

A bench stood beside the rock, quietly shedding its skin of *Relentless Olive* paint. Even though there was a bin, bottles lay strewn everywhere. Smashed glass caught the light of the stars and shone; a twin galaxy on the ground.

I slid off my rucksack, sat it on the bench and took out the tear catcher. Even though I had a sinking feeling we'd had a wasted journey coming to Guiltree Hill, I'd thought it best to be prepared and had slipped it into my coat pocket. "Do you think Carline Deedclathes senses we're here?" My legs started to tremble. The stars spun and blurred as though the earth was rotating on fast forward. I stole a furtive glance towards the path to safety and Saltbay.

"She'll be as dead as a dodo. We should check the stone for markings," said Moonzy as she trooped off to explore the other side of the rock.

"Why?" I asked Skaw.

"It's a trademark of witches – they're always vandalizing stuff with weird signs." He nodded wisely as I approached the boulder. The closer I got, the more it loomed over me. It must have taken all the townspeople of Saltbay to move it. I placed my hand against the stone, my fingers turning *Muted Fuchsia* in the cold. I tried hard not to imagine what it must have been like for Carline Deedclathes being buried alive.

Something tapped my foot and I leapt back, snapping my head down. Skaw shot off my hat, vanishing into a clump of grass at the base of the rock.

"It's only me!" squeaked Moonzy, waving her paws.

"Would you not do that!" I yanked my hat over my ears. "In case you haven't noticed I'm a little tense at the moment."

"There's nothing there." Moonzy bounded up on to my shoulder and over on to the rock, where she checked every inch of the top of it. Not detecting anything unusual, she sat, her tail flicking in annoyance.

I stared down at the grass but it was too long for me to spot where Skaw was.

Kneeling, I parted a clump and spied a small burrow under the boulder.

"Skaw? You there?" I hoped the hole wasn't inhabited by any creatures who considered worms to be gourmet delicacies.

Moonzy hopped on to my hat and slid down my arm, where she landed beside the tuft of grass. As she peered into the hole, she sneezed.

My mouth fell open.

The squirrel glared at me, wondering why I was gawping at her.

"You sneezed!" I said. "Doesn't this mean there's a witch nearby?"

Moonzy's eyes widened. "It's usually the case. . ."

Just at that moment Skaw's head appeared out of the burrow. "There's something on the underside of the stone, but there's no' enough light for me to see."

I dashed over to my rucksack, rifling through it for my phone and its torch. All of a sudden, I remembered Mum and Dad had confiscated it and I cursed out loud. Scanning the hilltop, something caught my eye in the bin, which gave me an idea.

The squirrel and the worm watched me intently, wondering what I was up to. I fished out the tinfoil lid of a takeaway carton and raced over to them, positioning it on the ground so the moon's rays reflected off it, flooding the hole with light.

"Great thinking, Coral!" Moonzy clapped her paws together.

Skaw wriggled back down under the rock. "A bit over to the right," he called out. "No. Your other right. That's it!"

Moonzy and I waited for him, hardly daring to breathe.

Skaw pushed up through the hole. "There's some writing on it. If Carline Deedclathes was buried alive, she could have done this."

I shuddered before I could stop myself.

The squirrel's whiskers stiffened. "What does it say?"

Skaw's eyes flicked up to the side as he recalled the words from memory. "*I am in the earth, right beneath here. A ring around me will bring me near. Say my name three times and I will appear. Don't place me back, or it will cost you dear.*"

"It's definitely a spell. That'll explain why I was..." Moonzy erupted with another sneeze, making Skaw and me jump.

"It says not to put her back, except you told me in the library she has to return to her grave." I frowned at the worm, not sure the world of magic was making much sense to me.

"If you'd been buried for hundreds of years, got your pulse kick-started and were set free, would you want to end up under there again?" Skaw jerked his head towards the earth.

Moonzy sat up. "The spell says we need to draw a circle. Lyart told me they were powerful shapes often used in magic rituals. Oh! And if the line gets broken, the magic can't work any more. Or so he said." She pulled a face.

"What will we draw it with?" Skaw bit his lip.

I hurried over to the bench and reached into the

patch of brambles, bringing out a discarded tin of the *Red Riot* spray paint, which rattled as I shook it.

"Brilliant! You can do it, Coral." Moonzy pointed to the stone.

"Why *me*?" I said, in a way that made me sound half my age.

"It would take the worm about forty years and you're an artist – I saw what was inside the sketch pad in your room. Once it's finished, Coral, say her name three times and then we'll wait for Carline Deedclathes." Moonzy brushed her paws together, as though it was a job well done.

"You have a way of making this sound as simple as baking a cake," I said, gripping the can of *Red Riot* spray paint. Some of it leaked out of the nozzle, on to my fingers. Although most people associated red with danger, Roman generals would paint themselves head to toe in the colour if they won a battle, and right at this moment, I liked the idea that red was seen as being victorious. A thought occurred to me. "I suppose I'll have to collect the tears from Carline Deedclathes too?" My voice was as taut as a guitar string the second before it snaps.

"Slightly tricky for me to do without arms," said Skaw.

Moonzy sucked her teeth. "You're taller and can reach her eyes better."

"What if she doesn't weep?" I asked, putting my hands on my hips.

Skaw shrugged. "She's being brought back to life by a girl, a worm and a stuffed squirrel. That's enough to reduce anyone to tears."

My skin thickened with goosebumps.

Skaw tapped my foot to get my attention. "Witches can be touchy at the best of times. This one is bound to be raging after being dead for so long."

"Skaw, do you have any other pearls of wisdom you'd care to share with us?" I picked him up and marched over to the bench where I perched, holding him in the palm of my hand at eye level.

"The witch will be way cleverer and can easily outsmart you, and if this goes pear-shaped, there will be no use in running because she'll be a million times faster."

I slumped on the seat. What had I been thinking? This task was going to be utterly impossible.

Skaw clocked the expression on my face. "Don't you give up now. I'm no' losing out on the chance to travel the world."

"Round of applause for Skaw, who wants to go on holiday with his beastly bestie." Moonzy's voice was as brittle as eggshells.

Skaw puffed his chest out. "I'm no' stupid. I've sussed you and Coral want to prevent Muckle Red from leaving the graveyard. As soon as we've gathered all the objects, you're on your own. I'll no' turn against my pal." Skaw flushed *Splash of Ketchup* as I plonked him on the bench.

"For a worm with eyes, you need to stop being so blind when it comes to Muckle Red," Moonzy snapped.

"Give him a break. He's worked hard to put the past behind him. He's a new man, an upstanding citizen, who on release from Halloway will devote his free time to charity work. Mark my words," said Skaw.

Moonzy flattened her ears and curled her tail in tight.

"Are you OK?" I could tell she was upset.

The moon highlighted scratches on the squirrel's pupils. "I wish Lyart was here. He'd have known exactly what to do," she said. "I'm just worried about him, that's all."

I hated the thought of Muckle Red holding him captive somewhere in Halloway graveyard. I could only pray he hadn't been harmed. "Lyart means the world to you, doesn't he?"

"It feels weird him not being with us – although I can still hear his voice jabbering away in my head, telling me what to do, which is kind of comforting and a little bit annoying."

Skaw rolled his eyes.

I smiled, thinking about my friend Isla. I loved her to pieces, even though she bugged me half the time too. I wouldn't have it any other way.

"If it's not too rude asking – what happened to Lyart? He's very young to be a ghost – and for you to be a poltergeist too."

"We got sick from an illness called Black Belly Fever."

"I'm sorry to hear this, Moonzy." I watched as her nose quivered. "Were you and Lyart friends before?"

"No, he saved me from some groaner goblins at Halloway and we've been inseparable ever since. He really does make the graveyard a safer place for everyone. This is the first time he's not been able to keep an eye on Muckle Red – he'll be beside himself with worry."

As I patted the squirrel's back gently, I pictured Gran smiling at me – the way she would when I came through the door after school and my heart floated like a helium-filled balloon that had been let go of in the park.

I had to give this a shot – for both of our sakes. "C'mon, let's do this."

Moonzy grinned at me, her nylon whiskers curling up at their ends.

I got to my feet and strode towards the boulder. Thankfully there wasn't much of a breeze and the ground was well-trodden, making it flatter than a sand dab fish. A circular path already existed around the stone, so I decided it would be best to follow it. As I pressed the top of the nozzle, spray hissed out of the can, coating the grass in a fine mist of *Red Riot*. The line was a bit wobbly in places; however, under the circumstances, it was the best I could manage. When I'd finished, I placed the nearly empty can on the bench.

"Well done. Great job." Moonzy carried Skaw over and dropped him next to the thin line. He squirmed out of her reach and then pulled himself up straight.

"Um. What should I do?" I bit my lip.

"Walk around the circle saying her name. You've got this, Coral!" Moonzy peered over at me.

I tried to speak, but I couldn't. I spluttered, my eyes watering. I remembered the words Lyart had said to me in the graveyard about breathing slow and steady to calm me down. When my lungs started to fill and my airways opened, I began to walk, calling out the witch's name.

My heart thudded faster than a dripping tap.

A cloud smudged the moon. Pushed by the breeze, a crisp packet flipped over like a winning card being played at a poker game.

I froze on the spot, not daring to move a muscle. After ages had passed, I let my breath out, ready to call it a night. I longed to be tucked up in my bed, cosy and safe.

Moonzy pursed her lips as though she was thinking really hard. "Lyart told me bad magic could work the opposite way from good magic."

"That explains everything, cloth ears." Skaw's body sagged.

Moonzy tutted. "What I mean is, maybe you should try it again, except walk anticlockwise this time?"

I had never dabbled in magic before, so I was prepared to give it a go. Doubting it would work, I strode the other way around the stone, saying the witch's name loud and clear.

Carline Deedclathes.

Carline Deedclathes.

Carline Deedclathes.

Moonzy and Skaw squinted nervously at the shadows.

Just as I was poised to kick at a juice carton in frustration, I heard a loud crack.

The ground shook and I lost my balance. The grass was damp under my hands and soaked the knees of my leggings.

The boulder rolled over, its underside alive with

insects. They showered down on to the grass where they swarmed, searching for cover.

Moonzy flicked the earwigs away with her tail and Skaw wrestled with a couple of centipedes. I whipped my scarf off and used it to sweep the woodlice from my legs.

The boulder halted as it reached the edge of the hill. Without warning, it crashed down, causing the bench to flip over and the bin to topple, spewing out its contents in fright.

Moonzy wrung her paws together. Skaw didn't once take his eyes off the bare patch of earth.

As I stood, a movement caught my eye.

A figure, silhouetted by an astonished moon, scuttled sideways up the side of the boulder on its hands and feet.

The squirrel and worm followed my gaze and gasped.

As the figure stretched, small pieces of decayed dress fluttered down like stunned moths. Carline Deedclathes shook herself, waking up every inch of time-withered flesh. She howled with anguish, lifted a straw-thin arm and pointed her finger towards the roof of the universe. Stolen moonbeams touched her curled nail and sparks flew. Her body lit up, reminding me of a crooked statue on a town square.

I clutched the tear catcher and inched forward. Just as I did, Carline Deedclathes shot into the sky faster than a satellite, scarred the face of the moon as she streaked across it, and vanished.

Moonzy was lost for words.

"That went well." Skaw batted away a woodlouse with force.

Something whistled through the air. As I craned my head up to see what it was, I heard a thud.

Moonzy and Skaw's mouths opened.

There, behind me, stood Carline Deedclathes.

Her hair hung in her face: the same pale yellow as grass that has been trapped under a plant pot, starved of sunlight. Carline Deedclathes's skin was leathery and earth-stained. Her eyes stared out, unblinking, reminding me of some never-before-seen creature from a specimen jar in a museum. What was left of her dress was as fragile as leaf skeletons.

"I need to know *why*." All the tendons stuck out on her neck. "*Why* have you done this?"

I teetered back from her, my heel grazing the edge of the *Red Riot* circle.

Carline Deedclathes made her eyes as narrow as wall cracks, searching for long-forgotten memories. She brought her hands up to her head and screamed. Clouds swirled and the tide raced out to sea. "My sisters: my poor, dreary sisters." Carline Deedclathes's eyes filled up with *Devil's Cape Black* water.

I hesitated, unsure what to do.

Skaw nodded his head vigorously, egging me on.

If I didn't get the tears, Lyart would never be freed, I'd lose the chance to be with Gran and children's lives would be at risk.

I whipped out the catcher, leaned forward and pressed it against Carline Deedclathes's cheek. A tear rolled into the tube, sliding down the side of the glass.

The witch growled and slapped my hand away. The tear catcher slipped from my fingers, twirled through the air and hit a stone, shattering into tiny fragments.

A cloud shielded the moon and shadows sneaked over the hilltop towards us.

Carline Deedclathes's eyes gleamed the same way

as wrecking lamps. She grabbed my wrist with coin-cold fingers and hauled me towards her. "Taking my tears can only mean one of two things: you're making a spell to extinguish dragon fire or you wish to free Muckle Red from Halloway. And you don't have what it takes to slay dragons."

Fear rubbed against all my nerve endings until they frayed.

Moonzy let out an almighty sneeze.

The witch's head cracked all the way round to look behind her. Carline Deedclathes let go of me, whirled over to the squirrel, and returned with her fingers wrapped around Moonzy's neck. I could tell from Moonzy's grimace the witch was hurting her.

Skaw flattened himself against the grass, desperate to make himself invisible.

"Why would you be wanting Muckle Red to escape from the graveyard?" demanded the witch.

Anger burned its way up my insides, barrelling past my stomach, heart and lungs. "You had a chance to keep Muckle Red inside Halloway graveyard, but instead you've made it possible for him to break free! It has to be one of the most useless spells ever cast."

The witch snorted and another tear squeezed out from her eye, leaving an inky line down her face. "Every spell has its purpose." Her voice was low, as though it came from somewhere deep inside her belly. She paced backward and forward so briskly, the ground was worn into mud. "Nippit Nebs. Bogle-Bo. Hellaine. Madrilda." Carline halted, clutching her stomach, as though suffering a wave of pain. "Those were the names of my sisters who lost their lives because of Muckle Red." Tears flowed freely; she wiped them, smearing *Devil's Cape Black* across her cheeks.

The shards of the tear catcher twinkled on the ground and I cursed myself.

"He set me up by stealing hearts and making people think it was the dark magic of witchcraft. Before the villagers captured me, I made sure Muckle Red suffered for what he had done; locked in a coffin, to be trapped in the graveyard until the Hallow moon would show."

Moonzy ceased struggling and hung limp.

I lunged to grab the squirrel but the witch spun out of reach faster than whirlwinds. Carline Deedclathes tensed with rage. "It was the townspeople of Saltbay who put my sisters to death, not Muckle Red. So, I gave him a chance to once again walk amongst them, because of what they did to me and my sisters."

"You really wouldn't care if he killed again? Especially after you know how it feels to lose loved ones?" I cried out.

A smile played on her *Oil Slick* lips. "If you gather the objects that release him, the deaths will be your fault, not mine." Carline careered over to the circle, hacking at the line with her heel, leaving a huge hole in it.

I stared at her. Moonzy had mentioned circles were powerful shapes used in rituals – except only if the line remained unbroken. The witch was making sure the magic couldn't work any more!

I flicked my eyes over to Skaw, but he'd vanished. My heart felt as though it had been kicked. He'd said it himself that he wouldn't turn on Muckle Red, and now with Moonzy captured, he'd left me on my own, to deal with Carline Deedclathes.

The witch raised Moonzy up in a way that made me shiver.

"Please, don't harm her," I pleaded.

Carline Deedclathes stared at me the same way a snake does before it strikes. She flicked her nails, *Orange Blast* sparks fizzing out from the tips of them.

A jagged line appeared by my feet, which widened into a yawning chasm, swallowing up grass, pill packets, coffee cups, a cider bottle and chip wrappers. The witch flung the squirrel headfirst into the crevasse.

"*Moonzy!*" I screeched.

Before I could leap in after her, the ground quaked, as the hole closed itself up.

Moonzy had been sealed in deep below the earth!

I saw red.

Carline Deedclathes should be inside the circle; it had raised her up and I was certain it had something to do with putting her back where she belonged.

I shoved her with every single ounce of anger I had in me. She twisted to the side, but I managed to catch her shoulder. The witch staggered backwards into the circle and fell, but immediately rose straight back on to her feet, as though hoisted up by invisible strings.

I sprinted over to the can of spray paint. If I could close the gap in the circle with it, the magic would work again.

Sparks shot out from Carline Deedclathes's fingertips and there was a rustling noise. The blackberry bushes sprang to life, their branches hurtling through the grass towards me. I dropped the spray paint and gasped as they wound their way over my legs and waist. Each time I went to kick them off, thorns pricked me. The brambles entwined my arms and neck, dragging me into the centre of the circle, where Carline Deedclathes was waiting.

"One day they'll dig under the stone and it'll be your bones they'll find, not mine."

I tried not to picture the rock rolling over the top of my grave.

Lyart had said not to underestimate Muckle Red, but a world with Carline Deedclathes in it would be an equally dangerous one. We had been idiots bringing her back without knowing how to reverse the spell.

The witch lifted her hands and wiggled her fingertips. The brambles started pulling me downwards, towards the grass, the thorns needling my skin as I sank to my knees.

I thought of Gran and how much I had wanted to see her one last time.

All of a sudden there was a flare of light, which hadn't come from Carline Deedclathes. The line of the circle was glowing *Molten Metal*. Shielding her eyes from the glare, the witch searched for the gap she'd made with her heel; however, the circle was once again complete.

I had no idea Carline Deedclathes could look even angrier.

I gulped.

The witch took a step towards me, but something flickered in her eyes. She hesitated for a split second, almost as if she was expecting me to say something.

That's when it hit me. Could the spell to return her to the ground be as straightforward as the one that raised her up?

"*Carline Deedclathes!*" I shouted out.

The witch brought her hands up to her face. The ground beneath her softened and churned into a squelching pool of mud. Carline Deedclathes's fingertips blazed as she pointed them at me, muttering words I couldn't catch.

Branches tugged at my legs and I fell. New bramble shoots gripped my throat and tightened. I tried to loosen them by moving my head from side to side, but they choked me, robbing me of my voice.

I closed my eyes.

"*Carline Deedclathes!*" I rasped.

The witch howled with so much loathing, every part of me quivered. Her arms flailed as she sank up to her knees in the sludge. It was as though the grave was slowly reclaiming her.

If I could only say her name one final time.

A branch snaked into my mouth, scratching my tongue. The vines sliding over my nose and cheeks glistened with tears. I couldn't breathe.

The stars swam. I tried to move but was held fast. I thought about Mum and Dad, and how much they'd already been through with losing Gran.

Gran had told me there wasn't anything I couldn't do if I put my mind to it.

I bit down as hard as I could on the bramble branch until it broke, and spat the pieces out. More shoots pushed against my face; I tilted my head as far back as it could go, thorns pressing into my scalp. I opened my mouth at the side, inhaling the tiniest bit of air. The vine encircling my ribs tightened and my ears rang. The edges of my vision blurred.

"*Carline . . . Deedclathes!*" It came out as barely a whisper.

The witch sank up to her neck in the gloopy muck. Exhausted, she kept as still as the night, watching me the same way as a wild animal does from a trap.

The shoots around my neck, face and chest loosened and my body heaved as I filled my tender lungs. I yanked at the branches, trying to untangle myself.

"I never meant for Muckle Red to leave Halloway," Carline Deedclathes wailed. "Let me go. I'm the only one who can end this for good."

I crawled out from the pile of brambles. Slowly, I got to my feet, my eyes never leaving hers for a second. "There are enough bad things going on in this world without you being in it. I'm going to do what you should have done in the first place. I'm going to stop Muckle Red from harming any more kids."

A groaning noise made my head snap round.

"Now would be a good time to leave the circle, Coral," said a strained voice. "Cannae hold this much longer."

That's when I saw him. Skaw was coated head to tail in *Red Riot* spray paint and had plugged the hole in the circle with his body. It had been the worm who had made it possible to reverse the spell. More radiant than an electric cooker ring, he started to flicker, like a bulb on the blink.

I peeled the last of the brambles off and stepped outside the circle.

As the mud reached her chin, Carline Deedclathes's voice prickled with hatred. "If you want the bones, follow the path to Greystoor Caves and Sully Tarn." Her eyes were full of cunning as she was dragged under the earth. Bubbles appeared on the surface, the only clue she had ever been here.

There was a giant crack and the boulder rolled over and lowered itself on the bare patch of earth, sealing her grave. It rocked backward and forward, settling itself once again to guard the witch.

Skaw lay flat out on the grass.

I crawled over to him. "Thought you'd done a runner."

"I'm a worm. No' an athlete."

I gazed at Skaw. I'd misjudged him. Just because he was small didn't mean he was useless. "I wouldn't be here if it hadn't been for you. Thank you."

The worm avoided my eyes. "Didn't do it for you. I did it so Muckle Red and I could travel the world together. Except that's no' going to happen now because you failed to get the tears. And no' that I'm complaining, but we've just lost Mad Moonzy into the bargain, which is going to slow us down."

Skaw's words stung worse than scorpions because he was right; I'd made a mess of everything.

I hoisted myself to my feet and staggered over to the rock. I clawed at the earth with my fingers. "Moonzy? Can you hear me?"

"She's under ten tons of rock and soil, Coral. I think you're being a tad on the optimistic side."

"Maybe we could raise Carline Deedclathes up again so that we can get Moonzy out?" I suggested.

"Are you joking? Have you completely lost your marbles?"

The clouds melted away and the moon and stars dazzled, their light colouring the sea *Midnight Blue* and crowning the waves with *Crystal White* crests.

My tears pushed the grit and bits of bramble leaves off my face.

There was no way I could leave without Moonzy.

A noise from the rock made me sit up straighter than lamp posts.

"Why is it witches never die?" Skaw groaned.

There it was again: plastic scraping against stone.

I limped forward, eyeing the boulder warily.

Something moved under the soil at the edge of the rock. A flattened piece of plastic poked out from the ground. It crackled and popped, until it had reshaped itself into a cider bottle. "Do you think you could give me a hand? Some of us have just been squished by a giant boulder," said the bottle.

Skaw and I glanced at each other.

"*Moonzy?*" I shrilled.

"Who else?" said Moonzy.

I knelt and brushed the earth off her. At the very bottom of the bottle, I spotted some *Devil's Black Cape* liquid sloshing around inside.

Skaw whispered, his eyes practically out on stalks. "Is that what I think it is?"

"That would be a big fat *yes*," said Moonzy, her ears swivelling. "That witch nearly got me good and proper."

"I'm so glad you're OK." I'd never hugged a bottle before; her plastic sides crumpled. "I really thought we'd lost you."

"Is the witch. . .?" Skaw nodded his head over in the direction of the stone.

"I can safely say Carline Deedclathes has been returned to her final resting place. I was lucky to get the tears." The bottle trembled. "She tried to take me down with her."

I picked Moonzy up and searched for my rucksack. I tightened the bottle's lid so Carline Deedclathes's tears wouldn't spill out and rolled Moonzy up in my scarf. I placed the bottle inside the bag, with the top sticking out the side of it. She must have been bone-weary because she didn't utter another word.

I returned for Skaw and tucked him into the brim of my beanie hat as I tramped across the grass to the path. We'd collected the witch's tears: now all we had to do was find the cannibal bones and a wrecker bird. I gritted my teeth, more determined than ever to talk to Gran before she became heavenbound.

CHAPTER 12

The last rays of the sun flooded into the kitchen, turning Mum's hair *Garnet Glory*. The washing-up liquid frothed up into bubbles as she swished her hand under the water, her *Pool Party* nail varnish making her hand look like a mermaid's. The suds slopped over the side of the bowl as she slid the plates in.

When I'd eventually got up this morning, I'd hobbled out to the garden and filled a jam jar with earth and compost for Skaw. I'd checked God's dish too, but the food was still untouched. I glanced up at Miss Mirk's windows, expecting to see her eye peering out at me through the hole in her blind. I was convinced she was hiding God, and although I had other more pressing things to deal with first, he was still very much on my mind.

Moonzy, Skaw and I had argued in hushed whispers all morning. Carline Deedclathes telling us where to find Sully Tarn was a mixed blessing. Skaw and I were grateful we knew where to go now, but Moonzy was more cautious, worried it might be a trap.

Mum waffled on about giving a customer a free makeover because she had walked past the counter with a sad face.

The dishcloth became soggy as I finished drying the cutlery. I wasn't sure what was worse: bringing Carline Deedclathes back from the dead or searching a cave inhabited by a cannibal for bones.

My stomach twisted the same way as tangled bedsheets on a washing line.

"You're quiet." Mum shoved the griddle that Gran and I used to cook pancakes on into the water. When I was younger, we'd make a batch of round ones and with the last of the batter, she'd let me do squiggles and letters. There really wasn't anything more delicious than hot pancakes.

Mum peered at me. "Are those scratch marks on your neck?"

I touched my skin. "Managed to get caught in some bushes searching for God." I tried not to imagine the expression on her face if I confessed I'd come close to being throttled by brambles because of stealing tears from an irate witch.

She paused. "You get your clumsiness from your gran; she was forever tripping on the lawn."

"She always said it was because she wanted to give the grass a hug."

Mum and I smiled at each other as she handed me the griddle. She plonked a pan into the basin, scrubbing it hard. "Your dad told me you went to the library yesterday."

"My book was overdue." I put the griddle away in the cupboard.

Mum filled the pan with water and put it to the side of the basin to steep.

"I think you were really brave. I know how special

the place was to you and your gran." She wiped around the sink with a cloth and then attacked the kitchen table, sweeping the crumbs up into her hand. The bin lid clanged against the radiator and the crumbs showered into it as she brushed her hands together.

"I'm dreading going to the hairdresser's. Your gran always sat next to me, being the life and soul of the place. The last time we were there, she was getting everyone to show off their tattoos." Mum grinned at the memory and then it faded with her next thought. "My hair will be down to my ankles before I can face going back."

"I could come with you, if you want?" I slung the wet dishcloth over the radiator and pulled a fresh one out of the drawer. It had a picture of Brad Pitt on it and Gran would say there was nobody she'd rather dry the dishes with.

"That's lovely of you, Coral." Mum touched my arm in a gentle way that showed she was grateful and leaned against the kitchen worktop. "Nothing makes a room emptier than wishing she's going to be in it. I keep expecting to find one of her notes on the kitchen table or to step over a pile of weeds she's left at the bottom of the steps." Mum fought hard to keep her voice steady.

I wanted to tell Mum the truth, to explain it was my fault Gran had died, and it would be such a relief because keeping this all to myself was making me feel as if I could burst at any second.

The dishcloth dropped to the floor.

"Coral?" said Mum.

The breath I was holding in escaped. I pushed the thought from my mind. Thanks to Lyart, I knew Gran hadn't crossed over to heaven yet, which meant she was still here.

"I think wherever we are, Gran will not be far away from us." I bent to pick up the dishcloth.

Mum's mouth opened slightly. She blinked twice; her *Deep Ocean* eyeliner flicked perfectly out at the sides, as though she had drawn it on with a ruler. "That's such a lovely thought, Coral." She tucked my hair behind my ear but it didn't stay there for long. "I could talk to Dad, if you want? I'm sure he wouldn't mind if you met up with Isla and your pals for a little while on Halloween? You've been through so much this past week."

You wouldn't be so lovely to me if you knew the truth.

My insides squirmed like maggots.

"I'm not really in the mood," I mumbled. I'd give anything to hang out with Isla and have a laugh with my friends, but on the night of Halloween, I had to stop Muckle Red from escaping the graveyard. "Mum?"

"Yes?"

"Can I have my phone back?"

"Nice try. Not until Monday. Come on, I think we've earned ourselves a cup of tea." She clicked the kettle on. "Away and see if there's something good on the telly."

"Would you mind if I went to my room?" Moonzy, Skaw and I had to prepare for the night ahead. And besides, I hated watching TV in the lounge now. Gran used to guard the remote and change channels halfway through a programme if she got bored, making us all mad at her. I would give anything for her to do this again.

"Are you all right?" The teabags swung in the air above the cups.

"I'm tired, that's all."

"Missing someone can be exhausting, Coral. You be sure and get a good night's sleep." Mum rubbed my back. I avoided her gaze, feeling awful about lying to her.

Just before I left the kitchen, I stole a last look at her standing on her tiptoes, sneaking her hand into the biscuit tin. I hoped I would make it out of Greystoor cave, alive, to see her again.

CHAPTER
13

The path to the cave was well-worn and steeper than slides. My footsteps made a hollow thud on the ground, which was studded with *Wolf Grey* smooth stones. To the right of us, the hill changed into a gorse-clad cliff and dropped sharply to the shore. As we began our descent, the waves rushed into the inlet below.

The cider bottle stuck out the side pocket of my rucksack. Moonzy cleared her throat in a way that indicated she was going to say something she knew might not be received too well. "Coral?"

One slip and we'd be taking the shorter, more lethal route to the cave.

"Mmm?" I kicked a stone, which clacked twice before vanishing over the side of the cliff.

"I can't shake the feeling something horrible is going to happen. Carline Deedclathes is not exactly going to be winning a prize for being Good Samaritan of the Year."

"You're no' wrong there," piped up Skaw, who was tucked into the fold on my beanie hat.

I hated that I kept on seeing Carline Deedclathes's eyes before she was sucked back into her grave. They would haunt me for the rest of my life. "Moonzy, what the witch said is all we've got to go on. I wish things were different, but we don't have much choice in the matter." I scratched an itchy spot on my head through my hat. I didn't like this one little bit either.

"I'm a plastic bottle, which is going to make tiptoeing around a cave searching for bones a little tricky." Moonzy sighed, exhausted.

"Can you no' just be you; I mean the real, earthbound you, and no' a stuffed squirrel or a bottle?" Skaw chewed on his bottom lip.

"You sound exactly the same as Lyart. I prefer being other things," she answered, her voice flatter than a skimming stone.

I hoped Lyart was OK wherever he was and that he wasn't going out of his mind with worry. I hoisted up the rucksack. "Skaw has a point, Moonzy. It might be a lot easier on you, if you were just yourself."

The bottle's sides cracked, giving me and Skaw a fright.

"I've been so many other things for so long, I'm not even sure I know how to be me." Moonzy sounded close to tears.

I stopped dead and plucked the worm off my hat. "Skaw, Moonzy would feel a lot better if you could just tell her where Muckle Red has hidden Lyart?"

Moonzy's plastic sides crinkled as she listened in.

"Do you think my head buttons up at the back? If I tell you, you don't need to collect the objects and Muckle Red can't leave the graveyard." Skaw pressed his lips together, emphasizing the point that he wasn't going to say another word on the matter.

"Thanks. Really helpful," muttered Moonzy.

"You're welcome," barked the worm.

I placed Skaw on my hat and stepped off the path on to the shingle beach. The waves charged towards me, narrowly missing my feet.

Facing us, at the end of the short cove, was a triangular cliff of *Grizzle Flint* stone topped with grass. At the very bottom of it was a narrow entrance. Fallen boulders crowded outside Greystoor cave, as though eager to catch a glimpse of Sully Tarn.

The thought of a cannibal creeping up on us set my nerves on high alert.

"We have a problem." Skaw was gazing straight ahead.

"*What?*" Moonzy and I both said at the same time.

"The tide's coming in."

This was a disaster! If we didn't get a move on, the cave entrance would be completely cut off by the rising waters.

Skaw started to quake uncontrollably. "W-we could return. When the tide is out."

"Everything all right there, Skaw?" asked Moonzy, sensing his hesitancy.

There was a pause. "Cannae swim," he confessed.

"Of course," said the bottle. "It's where you

always spot a worm – drowned in a puddle after the rain."

"If you're no' going to change into yourself, could you turn into something useful like a boat or a canoe or something?" The worm's voice quivered.

"Do you see one handily bobbing on the waves? There's your answer, then."

I took my rucksack off, lifted out Moonzy and placed her on the shore. The witch's tears were safe, as I'd poured them into an empty lip balm pot at home and hidden it in my wardrobe. I had rifled through the cupboard under the kitchen sink for a torch, but couldn't find one. The only thing I could think of to use were Gran's matches. Whenever she'd had a bath, she would fill the room with candles because she always swore their light made anyone look half-decent in the nude.

Fishing out the matches, I stuffed them into the pocket of my sweatshirt. Having something of Gran's with me felt as though it could somehow bring me luck. Lastly, I took off my coat. If I had to swim back from the cave, the wool might become so waterlogged, the weight of it could drag me under.

I shuddered as the breath of the sea whirled around me. I was so shattered each strange noise or swish of swaying grass became Sully Tarn stalking us.

Gran had told me I could make a difference by choosing one thing I believed in to fight tooth and nail for. I focused on the task ahead, like a telescope sharpening a faint blur in the night sky into a star. I wanted Gran to know how sorry I was, and for this to happen I was going to have to fetch the cannibal bones.

My heart banged out of rhythm. "Moonzy, you could make too much noise in the cave so you can be the lookout. Skaw, you can help me search for bones. It'll be dark, so I've got matches in case of an emergency, but I'd rather we didn't use them, as it could alert Sully Tarn that we're there. Any questions?"

"Being an earthworm, I'm extra sensitive to heat." Skaw nodded his head.

Moonzy and I gawped at the worm, waiting for him to explain himself further.

"It means if Sully Tarn is close by, I'll know," he huffed.

"That's brilliant, Skaw." I accidentally pictured a

cannibal standing next to us in the cave and shivered. "Listen, you two. I know Carline Deedclathes hasn't sent us here out of the kindness of her heart – so we are going to have to keep our eyes peeled. We have her tears, don't we? This has got to be easier. We go in, grab a bone and get out."

"In. Grab a bone. And out," chanted Moonzy and Skaw under their breaths.

I stuck the bottle in my sweatshirt pocket and checked Skaw was secure in the fold of my hat before picking my way along the shore.

The tide powered in, slapping my legs, and when it raced out, it sucked the stones from underneath my feet. The relief of reaching the rock pools was short-lived. Polished by starlight and booby-trapped with slippery fingers of seaweed, it was near impossible to keep my footing. I clambered over the uneven surfaces, wincing as limpets and whelks crunched under my feet, seaweed bladders popped and barnacles, sharper than teeth, cut my skin whenever I fell.

The waves behind us thundered in faster and stronger. As they pummelled the rocks, spray flew up, soaking me. My nose filled with the smell of salt, reminding me of fresh blood. I clawed my way over the last of the boulders, overjoyed to finally arrive on dry land. I stood, wiping my face with my sleeve to stop the seawater stinging my eyes. My chest heaved up and down, and my body trembled.

The cliff loomed over us, sprouting old bird nests from its crevices. Gannet droppings dripped down the stone, as if pots of *Wedding Veil* matt emulsion had been accidentally spilled. Spindly trees gripped on to tiny cracks and *Ochre 2* lichen blossomed over the rock.

My tread became deer-quiet as we approached the entrance, a low yawning mouth in the cliff, poised to swallow us in one gulp.

I placed Moonzy to the side of the opening.

"Give us a warning if the tide gets too high or Sully Tarn appears." I gave her a weak smile.

The bottle dipped its top.

To the left of us, there was a small hole in the rock. I didn't bother to check it; if I couldn't slip in or out of it, neither could Sully Tarn.

Crouching, I stepped inside, straining my ears,

but all I could hear was the swell of the sea. I smelled bird poop, fish and rotting seaweed.

The cave was darker than a power cut; I kept to the right, my hand feeling my way along the wall. The rock started to slant inwards until it came together with the opposite side. I had to duck, careful not to bang my head, and squeezed through the gap at the bottom. I crawled on my hands and knees, small stones pressing themselves into my legs and palms, as we entered another chamber. I could no longer hear the waves – just my heart clunking against my ribs.

As I inched forward, I patted my foot lightly on the ground, hoping it would kick a piece of bone.

"Sk-aw?" I said, quieter than a whisper. "A-ny-thing?"

He leaned over the fold of my beanie hat. "Nope."

I moved on a couple of steps.

Up ahead, I heard a noise, similar to the soft tread of footsteps.

"*What was that?*" Skaw held his breath.

I fought the urge to cough. My nostrils flared and my throat tickled. Feeling dizzy, I clung to a narrow shelf on the rock, knocking dust off it, which fell to the ground the same way sugar spills from a bag.

As the sound echoed around us, I stumbled, my hat catching on something. My hand shot up to feel a tree branch, no thicker than a knitting needle, sticking out from the wall. I snatched my beanie off it and put it back on to my head.

I hoped Lyart wasn't being held, alone, in a place as horrible as this. I thought about his soothing words that had helped me to breathe properly again. The urge to cough left me and I inhaled. Thing was, I'd been so busy focusing on trying not to choke, I had no idea which direction I was going in. I felt around my head for Skaw, except he wasn't there. He must have been knocked off when my hat snagged on the branch.

I didn't want to be in this cave all by myself.

"Sk-aw?" My scalp bristled with fear.

"Aye?" said a voice right in my ear.

I let out a gasp.

"Calm your jets. I got knocked on to your shoulder."

"You scared me!"

"Eh, newsflash: I'm no' as terrifying as a cannibal. And you're heading the wrong way."

I swivelled and pushed on, only hoping if Sully Tarn was close, Skaw would be able to sense him.

It wasn't long before I heard another sound, close by – a high-pitched rush of air.

"Skaw?" I stood stock-still, petrified.

"Aye, sorry. That compost you're feeding me is awfully rich; it's giving me terrible wind."

"*Skaw!*"

"I said *sorry*."

I crept on, further into the cave.

A faint pitter-pattering noise halted me in my tracks. Sweat trickled down my spine, making me shiver. I was too hot and too cold all at the same time. "I don't think I can do this." I dug my fingernails into the palms of my hand, desperate to fight back the tears.

"Aye, you can. The tide is coming in fast, and in case you've forgotten, I cannae swim. I'm risking my life in the hope of a better one with Muckle Red. You just keep thinking of that wee granny of yours and carry on."

I wished I'd brought Moonzy instead. I picked up the pace, my right fist clenched for good measure.

Skaw twitched. "There's something up ahead."

"*What?*" It was hard not to screech it out loud.

The worm craned his neck, trying to see. "A light."

I inched forward, aware of a faint glow coming from an opening at the end of the corridor. When we got there, I mustered up all my courage to peep around the corner.

Skaw and I were astonished that the cave was bigger than the inside of the church. In the centre of the floor was a weathered rowing boat, which had been made into a table. On the bare rock wall hung a *Satsuma Punch* trawler net, covered in every size of fishing hook imaginable. Underneath it was a shopping trolley stuffed full of bags, shoes and clothing. A headless doll sat on top with its arms outstretched. Next to that, a tarpaulin sheet had been draped over an object.

At the side of the table, a fire crackled. Above it was a huge metal keg, suspended from the wall by iron chains. Giant plumes of steam whooshed out from it, billowing across the cave.

I scanned the floor for bones; there was nothing.

Skaw spoke quieter than Miss Mirk. "There are a couple of chambers off the main one; we'll need to check them out."

"Can you sense him?"

He shook his head. "Only the heat from the fire."

I stood and rounded the corner. Although the dark was terrifying, at least it had kept us hidden.

Stepping down into the cave, I waited for the steam to clear.

"Try the chamber next to the net." Skaw pointed his head in the direction of it. "Hurry!"

I darted across the floor, flattening myself against the rock. Once satisfied Sully Tarn wasn't in sight, I poked my head into the chamber, which was cooler and unlit.

I slipped into the blackness.

"Hold on, Coral! Wait!" Skaw went rigid.

I hesitated, reaching out for the damp rock to steady myself. That was when I felt someone else's fingers underneath mine.

I squealed.

A hand clapped over my mouth and my arm

was pinned behind me. As I struggled, the grasp tightened and I was lifted off my feet. My leg shot out to kick my captor but struck stone, bringing tears to my eyes.

"Yell and rocks will come down from the ceiling. You won't even know what has hit you." The man spoke as though his voice had rusted in the sea air.

I wondered if the noise of my thundering heart could make the entire roof collapse.

Sully Tarn pushed me into the cave and hauled me over to the tarpaulin sheet. He tore it off to reveal a cage and bundled me inside it. I darted to the far side, desperate to get away from him. The ground was smooth as sea glass and there were scratch marks on the rock. As my eyes travelled upwards, I noticed the bars were made from *Sail Cloth*–coloured bones, lashed together with fishing wire. I gasped, panic rising up in my chest.

Skaw had vanished from my shoulder. I hoped he hadn't been squashed in the scuffle. All the steam and shadows made it impossible to tell if he was on the floor. Maybe the thought of the tide rising had been too much for him and he'd scarpered!

Sully Tarn crouched to peer through the cage at me. "By the state of you, you've had quite the journey getting here. Quite the journey."

My soaking clothes clung limpet-tight to me. I brought my knees up and hugged them.

Sully Tarn's skin was paler than fish bones and his eyes were the same shade as *Pond Frost*.

Every part of me was paralysed with fear.

The cannibal walked over to the fire to put some wood on it. The flames crackled, licking the base of the keg. He emerged from a fresh cloud of steam to sit across from me. His hair was shaved to his scalp, which was criss-crossed with raised scars. He wore a *Bolt Grey* shirt under *Sunflower Yellow* oilskin dungarees. On his feet were a brand-new pair of *White Ash* trainers. Most people think the colour represents goodness and cleanliness, except I read in some parts of Asia, white is associated with death.

"What's your name?" He dug his heels into the ground and pushed his chair back.

My lips were as dry as dune sand. "Coral."

"How did you know I was here?"

"According to Saltbay Library you don't even exist." I tried and failed not to shake.

"In this world, it's better to be invisible." He let his chair drop and leaned on the tabletop. "The tide cuts the cave off; most people don't risk it. But you did. Why?"

"Carline Deedclathes said you'd be here." The door to the cage had been lashed shut with fishing line too.

"What did you do to upset her?"

I raised my eyebrows.

"She knows what I am. Think you do too."

I shifted uncomfortably. "I brought the witch to life and then returned her to the grave."

He thought about what I'd said for a while. "My family goes back many generations – they despised Carline Deedclathes. Grand-Papa Tarn would have done away with her; however, the good townspeople of Saltbay got to her first. The witch accused him of killing some of the local children – she should have known we'd never only remove the hearts. Such a waste of good flesh. Unthinkable, really." Sully Tarn devoured me with his eyes for a second, as though I was a rack of ribs smothered in BBQ sauce.

Sweat trickled down the side of my face as I worked my way around each of the bars, pulling at the bones to see if any of them were loose.

Sully Tarn half cocked his head. "Nobody gets out of there alive, Coral."

I searched along the base of the cage for something I could use to cut through the wire, but there was only grit and dust.

"If you let me go," I said, "I won't tell a soul about you."

Sully Tarn shrugged. "Maybe you'd keep your mouth shut for a while – but me being here would eat away at you, and then you'd start fretting about the safety of your family and friends. The next thing you know, you'll have confided in one of your pals and the rumour would spread through the whole of Saltbay. Then people would start showing up, ruining everything. The only reason my family survived here for so long is because we're a secret. I was taught to cast the net far and wide when I'm hunting, and always cover my tracks."

I knelt and peered through the gaps at him. "My mum and dad know where I am and if I don't come home, they'll go to the police. I left my coat and bag on the beach, where they'll be easily found."

Sully Tarn studied me, carefully.

"It's the middle of the night. By the condition of your skin and hair, you've been well cared for, so I'll hazard a guess you sneaked out of the house and your parents are fast asleep and don't have a clue you're here."

My shoulders slumped. I was trapped like a fly in a web. Lashing out at the bars with my feet, I roared at the top of my voice.

The cannibal gazed up at the ceiling. "Silence! Or I'll come into that cage and do it for you myself."

I closed my mouth.

"You're the first child I'll have dined on in a while. You're far too good for the pot – boiling is for softening tough old flesh. Tonight, I'm going to have me a roast." Sully Tarn vanished off into the chamber at the rear of the cave.

"Pssst!"

My eyes swivelled down to the floor.

"Skaw!" I bellowed, before slapping my hands over my mouth. I flattened myself on the ground. "I thought you'd gone and left me."

"Why is it you always assume the worst of a worm?"

My eyes welled up; I'd never been happier to see him. "You've got to get me out of here."

"I'll try to gnaw through the wire. You'll have to distract him though, to buy me some time."

"Please, *please* hurry."

I pushed down the sick feeling inside me and willed my teeth to stop chittering. I had to do something; I was moments away from being served up as chops.

Sully Tarn reappeared with some salt and a carving knife, which he placed on the table.

"I guess I'd never imagined being alone when my time was up," I blurted out.

Sully Tarn's eyes glittered as he walked up to the cage. I saw his teeth, higgledy-piggledy like a shark's. "But you're not on your own, are you?"

In a flash, Sully Tarn ducked and his hand shot out to grasp Skaw. He pulled him back out through the cage bars, holding him between his thumb and forefinger. "You've got a worm for company."

Skaw bit Sully Tarn on the finger. The cannibal

flapped his hand so vigorously, the worm shot through the air, landing next to the trolley. Sully Tarn tore after Skaw, who had wriggled under a pile of clothes. He raked his way through them, determined to capture the worm.

With Sully Tarn's back turned, I kicked against the door of the cage – it still held strong. Skaw hadn't had enough time to chomp through the wire. In a flash, an idea came to me. I brought out Gran's matches and struck one. My ragged breath blew the flame out and I cursed. With shaking hands, I managed to light another, and held it under the nylon line, which blackened, withered and snapped.

Sully Tarn clambered to his feet, holding Skaw aloft in the air. "You'll make a tasty protein-packed starter. So you will."

The worm bared his teeth at him.

I gripped the bars; Sully Tarn had no idea I could get out of the cage.

The cannibal marched across to the keg and thrust Skaw out over it. The worm's shrieks were so piercing, dust rumbled down from the ceiling.

I clapped my hands over my ears. I'd never heard

such a sickening sound in my life. Skaw could have left, except he had stayed, attempting to rescue me. I had to do something to save him from the boiling water.

"What are the pair of you up to?" asked Sully Tarn.

"N-n-nothing! I'm just a worm!" shrieked Skaw.

"A worm trying to free a girl from a cage!" Sully Tarn narrowed his eyes. "What's going on? Tell me, otherwise you're for it!"

I smashed the door open and barrelled forward. "Let him go!"

Sully Tarn faced me, holding on to Skaw, his eyes widening for a second.

"We need one of your bones to stop an evil entity being released from Halloway graveyard," I barked.

"You're not leaving with any of my bones; it's evidence that'll lead back to me." Sully Tarn swung Skaw out over the bubbling water. Steam hissed and billowed past us. "Get back inside your cage or it's the end for the worm."

"Let Skaw go, otherwise I'll make sure every single person in Saltbay knows about you." I set my mouth in a thin line.

"Let him go?" Sully Tarn's lips twitched.

I crossed my arms in front of me to let him know I meant it.

Sully Tarn opened his hand and released the worm.

I watched in horror as Skaw disappeared into the keg.

It didn't matter Skaw couldn't swim; the liquid would be hotter than molten lava. There would be no way he could survive that.

"Why so sad?" Sully Tarn observed me with interest. "You told me to let go of the worm – I did what you asked."

I screamed at the top of my voice.

An avalanche of dust rushed down from the roof of the cave.

Sully Tarn dived towards me, knocking me flying. The full force of him landing on me flattened my lungs and I lost my breath.

"You're trouble, Coral," hissed Sully Tarn. "No wonder Carline Deedclathes wanted rid of you."

Just at that moment some rocks tumbled from the ceiling, the tip of a stalactite smacking him on the back of his head. His eyelids fluttered and he fell to the side. I wriggled out from under him and leapt to my feet.

I didn't want to, but I had to check inside the keg for Skaw. I stood on my tiptoes, waiting for the steam to clear, and peered into it, frightened of what I might find.

There, clinging on to a thick strand of seaweed stuck to the side of the pot, was the worm.

"Skaw!" I plucked him out of the water to safety. I rushed over to the table and laid him out.

His skin was the colour of *Cajun Shrimp*, but he blinked at me.

"Don't ever give me a fright like that again. I don't know what I'd do without you."

The worm's voice came out a whisper. "Thanks for telling him to let go of me."

"I didn't know he'd do it for real! Can you move?"

Skaw winced as he wriggled his tail. I ripped the sleeve of my top and wrapped him up in it. "The hurt you're feeling now won't be anything compared to the sting of the salt from the seawater."

Skaw's eyes widened.

"I know, I know – I'll try my best to keep you dry."

He shook his head.

"What? You don't trust me? I promise I won't let anything happen to you."

"Behind you!" he croaked.

Sully Tarn had propped himself up, woozily. I scooped Skaw up and shoved him into the fold of my beanie hat. Sully Tarn rose and lurched towards me, furious.

If we were to get out of here alive, there was no time to snatch a bone. I bolted towards the exit, where I charged blindly along the corridor. Hearing the thud of feet behind me, I collided into a solid wall of rock, pain shooting through my skull. Too terrified to cry out, I sank to my knees. As I dragged myself through the other side of the gap, a hand grasped my ankle, hauling me back. I lashed out with my other leg until there was a yowl of pain. I bucked with all my strength and scrabbled forward through the hole.

Without a bone, we'd lost the chance to release Lyart from his hiding place!

Careering out the cave, I seized the cider bottle and pelted towards the churning sea, which now covered the rock pools. It was so deep, I was going to have to swim ashore.

"Hey! Don't forget *me*!"

I spun round to see a skull perching on top of a plastic crate, clacking its jaws together.

"It's Moonzy!" Skaw rasped.

I eyeballed the bottle in my hand and then the skull. That was when it dawned on me; Moonzy had changed herself into one of the skulls of Sully Tarn's victims and we had the cannibal bones that we needed!

I bombed over to her, opened the empty bottle, dropped Skaw inside it and screwed the lid on as tightly as I could. If I had to swim, it would need to be watertight to keep Skaw safe.

"Moonzy, you're a genius," I said, flashing a grin.

I put both the skull and the bottle inside my sweatshirt and zipped it up.

A clattering sound made my head jerk up.

Sully Tarn was clambering over the rocks towards us, swinging a rope over his head. *Platinum* hooks flashed on the end of it as they twirled in the air.

I launched myself into the sea, the iceberg coldness squeezing the breath from my lungs. All of a sudden, something caught my sweatshirt and I was tugged back. A hook must have attached itself! If I couldn't get rid of it, I'd be landed like a fish. As I was reeled in towards the rocks, an almighty wave lifted me up and threw me down, sucking me under. The force of it snapped the line and I drifted free. Another hook splashed into the sea beside me. I yowled as it embedded itself in my hand, clawing at my skin as it was yanked sharply. A wall of water crashed over my head, and I rolled forward, losing all sense of which way I was facing. The last of my breath escaped from my mouth in *Silver Marlin* bubbles. Crashing against rocks, every bone in my body felt on fire. Weakened by pain, I gave one last push with my feet. My head shot up through the water and the beach came into view for the briefest of seconds. I flailed my arms, using my legs to propel me towards it. The sea coughed and I climbed high on a wave, before rushing forward at breakneck speed to be spat out on to the shore. I heaved myself over seaweed and shingle, checking behind me to see if Sully Tarn was following, but he'd gone. I unzipped my sweatshirt. Moonzy tumbled out and landed on top of a pile of driftwood – but the bottle had vanished.

It must have slipped out when I got hit by the wave!

I waded back into the sea, crying out Skaw's name. With these currents, the bottle could be halfway across the ocean by now.

"Don't risk your life for that wretched worm, Coral. He's not worth it," Moonzy hollered.

The waves knocked into me, making it impossible to get past them. I stifled a sob. Scaw had a misplaced loyalty to Muckle Red but I wouldn't have survived this far without him.

"Coral! Over here." Moonzy sped towards the water.

I waded in the direction of the skull, the waves trying their best to slow me down.

That's when I saw a glint of plastic. The bottle was tumbling on to the beach and being pulled back out to sea, again and again. I stooped and grabbed it, frightened to peer inside. If water had seeped into it Skaw couldn't have survived. I twisted the lid off and Skaw blinked up at me, his face *Sea Kelp* green.

"I'd never have forgiven myself if something had happened to you, Skaw."

The worm raised his *Slate in the Rain* eyes up at me. "Think I'm going to puke."

The relief we were all alive and safe swept through me stronger than undertows. I collapsed on the shore, unable to move.

As the part of the sky that touched the ocean blushed *Spiced Rum*, *Caramelized Peach*, *Soul Blue* and *Lantern Glow*, a thought occurred to me. I propped myself up on my elbow. "You guys, you know what this means?"

The skull and the worm glanced at each other.

"We've only got ourselves a wrecker bird to catch now."

A lone seagull cried out above our heads, crabs scuttled sideways, anemones closed their tentacles and fish dived deeper into the ocean's depths.

CHAPTER 14

"I'd rather be eaten by a cannibal." Skaw whacked my hand with his tail and then groaned. "It'd be less painful."

You'd think the worm would have been overjoyed we'd all made it back home, safe and sound.

"Hold still," I said, attempting to dab disinfectant on his wounds. He was lucky to have suffered only minor burns, after what had happened in the cave.

"If you don't do as she says, Skaw, it'll become infected with oozy pus and then you'll stink worse than roadkill and nobody will marry you because you'll be dead," said Moonzy, nodding.

Skaw squirmed on the tissue paper I'd laid down on the kitchen table. "That'd make your day, wouldn't it?"

The skull stayed silent, sniffed a cauliflower, took a nibble from it and spat it out. I'd placed her in the vegetable rack, in case Dad waltzed in unannounced as parents have a knack of doing. Mum had gone to work and Dad had written a note to say he'd only be twenty minutes. Thing was, I'd slept in and had no idea what time he'd left.

When I'd woken up, I'd checked God's bowl, but it was still full. It took all my willpower not to march straight round to Miss Mirk's, kick her door down and demand she handed him back. My grip on Skaw tightened at the thought.

"Ow! Do the world a favour; never become a nurse." Skaw stuck his nose in the air.

I held my hands up. "OK, I'm done. I'm stepping away from the ungrateful patient, although you heart me really."

Skaw opened his mouth to protest but I cut him

short. "I know: you only saved me because you want to get out of Halloway."

The worm tried to wriggle off the tissue, except it stuck to him. I put my finger on it so he could free himself.

I fetched a glass and opened the fridge.

"What do you suppose Sully Tarn will do?" asked Skaw.

"He knows we can blow his cover. I reckon he'll be long gone by now and good riddance to him." I poured out some cherry juice, spilling some as I remembered the hooks twirling in the air. It must have been how he'd caught his victims.

I closed the door and padded over to the table, sitting with care. There wasn't one part of me that didn't ache.

Skaw made his way past Mum's empty breakfast plate and peeped over the edge of the table at Moonzy. "By the way, where did the skull come from?"

"Remember the gap in the wall at the cave's entrance? Found a hoard of bones inside it. Thought the skull would be more useful than a sternum. Or a clavicle. Or a fibula." Moonzy shuddered. I could tell she was trying hard to forget what she'd seen.

"Just wait until Lyart discovers it was your quick thinking that helped to rescue him," I said, smiling. I was looking forward to seeing him again and it would make Moonzy so happy.

The front door opened.

I whipped Skaw away from the table's edge and wrapped him in the tissue. I leapt up and plonked a bag of carrots over Moonzy's head. As Dad walked into the kitchen, I yanked my sleeves down to cover my bruises.

"Oh, we're awake, are we?" said Dad, carrying his phone in one hand and a book in the other. "Met Mrs Shellycoat outside – she brought you this." The plastic cover squeaked under his fingertips. "And she said to say hello."

It must be the book on the wrecker bird! I was poised to leap up and snatch it when Dad placed it on top of the bread bin.

"I got a call from the vet, about a black cat which had been found without its collar. That's where I've been." Dad slipped his coat off, hung it over the chair and sat.

I searched his eyes for bad news.

"It wasn't God." Dad rubbed his face wearily.

I breathed out.

"This poor fellow had been found in a ditch, badly injured, and didn't pull though."

I hoped Miss Mirk hadn't laid a finger on God. I wished I could tell Dad I was certain she had the cat, but it would only stir up trouble between us. I was going to have to find solid proof Miss Mirk was hiding him.

"You OK?" He raised his head up.

"I'm sad for whoever lost their cat." I rested my chin on my hand.

Dad nodded. "Don't be too downhearted – we've still got hope." His beard had grown even thicker and darker, as if he was trying to hide behind it.

I offered a weak smile.

"I promised your mum I'd do a shop. Want to come? We could go for a stroll along the beach afterwards?"

If Gran had been here, that's what she would have suggested we do. Walk and talk and let the sea breeze blow any sadness away. My heart filled with a longing to see her.

I stared over at the library book. Time was running out to find the wrecker bird. Tonight was Halloween and there was still a chance I could talk to Gran.

"Think I'll stay and read instead," I said.

Dad's shoulders lowered in a way that meant he wasn't expecting my answer. "Right then. OK. I won't be long. Please don't go off anywhere – you're still grounded – and could you tidy away the breakfast things?"

I nodded.

Dad got up and grabbed the tissue Skaw was bundled up in and a peppermint teabag wrapper. The bin lid clanged open as he flung them in. He tied up the bag, which whistled as he pulled it out.

"I'll do that, Dad!" I didn't want Skaw to be crushed. I wasn't sure how much a vet would be able to do for a worm.

"Has the real you been kidnapped by aliens and replaced by an extremely helpful robot?" Dad exaggerated the astonishment on his face.

"Very funny."

Dad froze and then cleared his throat. "Now I know it really is you. Who else would leave a skull in the vegetable rack?"

The carrots had slid off Moonzy, who was now in full view, grinning at us.

I shrugged. "It was for Halloween."

Dad clenched his jaw. "Your mum had a word about you going out for an hour or two tonight with your friends. I'll think about it; however, I'm not promising anything. Do you understand?" He put on his jacket and checked his inside pocket for his wallet. "I'm away now. Want to move the head upstairs before Mum gets back, so she doesn't lose hers when she sees it?"

I didn't even hear the door closing behind him.

I pounced on the book.

"Oh no!"

Moonzy's skull popped up, sporting celery-leaf hair in a pixie cut. "What now?" she asked.

"*Mythical Birds of the World*. Wrecker birds don't even exist." I chucked it on the table. It skidded across the surface, upsetting an empty cup.

Moonzy and I heard a mumbling noise.

"I'd better let him out." I tipped my head in the direction of the bin bag.

"Shame," muttered the skull under her breath.

I marched over and undid the grey ties. My nose wrinkled as I searched through the rubbish for Skaw. Eventually, I found the tissue and brought him out. I unwrapped it, releasing him from his soggy, tea-stained prison.

"Have you no' learned a thing? If a bird, animal or object is mythical, it absolutely, positively exists," said Skaw.

I wiped the tea leaves and spaghetti sauce off my hands and then kicked the bin bag for good measure. More of its contents spilled on to the floor. "It's just we're so close. I couldn't bear it if we couldn't find the bird."

Skaw drew himself up to his full height. "Having a hissy fit isn't going to help."

I threw the spilled rubbish into the bag.

Moonzy launched herself off the vegetable rack and skidded to a halt under a chair. I picked her up, placed her on top of the book, and started to clear the table.

"I understand exactly how you feel, Coral. I

could burst with excitement at the prospect of finally seeing Lyart tonight! And if I thought it wasn't possible I'd EXPLODE, which would be really messy." Moonzy spun four times on the spot.

"Go and no' do that!" Skaw puffed his cheeks out. "Feel as if I'm back at sea."

Moonzy continued on. "Let's not dwell on everything that could go wrong. Let's believe something wonderful is going to happen."

"Would you stop with the airy-fairy claptrap? We need to get cracking." Skaw busied himself looking up the chapter the wrecker bird was in. Moonzy flipped the pages with her teeth and then flattened them by bouncing on the book. Once she'd scooted off it, Skaw started to read out aloud.

"*Wrecker birds were kept for their ability to sense bad weather approaching. The famous Scottish explorer Lachlan the Boneless kept two in a cage on board his ship and would release one if he suspected conditions at sea were changing for the worse. If the bird circled overhead or returned to ship, a storm would be fast approaching and the boat would sail to safety. If the bird flew in a straight line, the ship would follow, knowing the waters ahead were calm. On his last voyage, Lachlan ran out of food and feasted on one of the birds. When the surviving bird was released, bereft at the loss of its companion, it led the sailors straight into an approaching cyclone and all were lost at sea. It is said the bird only appears after a death and sings to bring comfort to all those lost in grief."*

"Maybe not a bird you can encourage into the garden with breadcrumbs?" offered Moonzy.

"We still don't know where to find one." I lobbed the butter into the fridge. Returning to the table, I pulled the book towards me. On the right-hand page was an illustration of the creature. Small, with a plump *Vintage Aubergine* chest, it had a crown of tiny *Marquis Orange*–tipped fan-like feathers on its head. Its *Saffron Thread* eyes were framed by an *Ebony King* eye mask and its tail was long and shimmered every colour of green imaginable.

I sat up. I'd seen those exact same tail feathers before. I hadn't been able to take my eyes off them as they had waved around on Miss Mirk's hat.

I jabbed my finger at the picture. "The bird! It was on my neighbour's head at Gran's funeral. Not the actual bird, but those feathers were. Miss Mirk has been stealing missing posters of pets and buying cat food when she doesn't have one, and I'm certain she's hiding God."

Moonzy's jaw dropped, clattering on to the table. Skaw and I had to give her a hand to reattach it.

"What are we waiting for? Let's go!" she said finally, waggling her mandible.

"We can't!" I wailed.

Skaw banged his head off the pepper mill.

"Why not?" Moonzy asked in a higher-pitched voice than mine.

"If Miss Mirk catches me in her house, she'll call the police, and Mum and Dad have enough going on without having to visit me in prison." I put the pepper out of the reach of Skaw and jumped to my feet. "Every Friday evening Miss Mirk goes to the bingo. I'll plead with Mum to let me meet my friends and she'll persuade Dad it's a good idea. We'll sneak into Miss Mirk's house, find the wrecker bird, search for God and then come here, so Mum and Dad think I'm home – and then we can climb out my window and take all the objects to the graveyard."

"If I'd hands right now, I'd so clap." Moonzy widened her eye sockets.

"No' to bring a downer to the proceedings, but there's the small matter of getting in to her house?" Skaw parked that thought with us.

That's when I remembered what I'd spied as I'd put God's poster through her door. "The latch on her front window was open," I said triumphantly.

"Ta-da!" Moonzy danced on the tabletop.

"It seems we have a chance at getting our hands on this bird after all." Skaw blinked as though pleased, and just for a second there was the hint of a smirk on his lips.

I was sure he'd be thinking about escaping from the graveyard with Muckle Red, except Lyart, Moonzy and I wouldn't let this happen. If Skaw knew how horrendous Muckle Red really was, he might not be so eager to leave with him.

Even though we now had a clue as to where the wrecker bird might be, the thought of having to see Muckle Red again wasn't a good one.

*

The Hallow moon near filled the whole sky, its light intensifying all the colours around us. It was hard not to be amazed at the hedge which glowed *Electric Eel* and the weeds as they flickered *Acid Green*: something the skull and the worm failed to notice.

A crowd of kids dressed as ghosts, monsters and witches stampeded past, shrieking at the tops of their voices. Moonzy, Skaw and I shrank into the shadows.

I checked my watch. Mum and Dad had given me exactly two hours before I had to be home. For a while, I wasn't even sure Dad would agree to it, but Mum told him I'd been shut inside all week, which wasn't healthy for a girl of my age, and that she was certain I could be trusted.

If I messed this up, there would be nobody left at home to fight my corner.

"I'm no' going in first." Skaw glared at me.

"Listen, Skaw, you're the smallest. If you slip in and the coast is clear, it means I can push the window up and we can get the wrecker bird."

"What if that gargantuan cat of yours is lying in wait?"

I flapped my hand in the air, dismissing his concerns. "You'll be fine. He's a really fussy eater."

"Come on, Skaw! Miss Mirk is an old lady. The worst she can do is hit you with her handbag or run you over with her shopping trolley. What's the problem?" Moonzy ground her teeth, impatiently.

Skaw snorted. "Every single time we think it's going to be easy, it turns out to be a total nightmare. And do we even know if she's at the bingo?"

My eyes avoided his. I couldn't be certain Miss Mirk had left the house as Mum had called me to the dinner table.

Skaw flushed *Red Riding Hood*. "This is the last time I'm sticking my neck out for you two. Do you hear me? The very last time."

Moonzy winked at me. I checked the coast was clear and opened the window a quarter of an inch for him to wriggle through. He halted to mutter something I once saw scribbled on a toilet wall in school, and then disappeared behind the net curtain. A few seconds later, the worm popped up. "All clear," he mouthed through the glass.

I flattened my hands against the window and

pushed it up. As the gap at the bottom widened, I worked my fingers underneath it. The window began to slide open and then jammed.

I picked up Moonzy and squeezed us through, my head emerging from the net curtains. My rucksack wedged itself and I had to wiggle from side to side, kicking my legs.

"Be careful! If the pot with the witch's tears breaks, we've had it," warned Moonzy.

"It's well wrapped up; don't worry." Landing in a heap, I let go of Moonzy, who smacked into a table leg.

"It's like watching clowns at work," muttered Skaw as I scowled at him, before tucking the worm into my hat.

The moonlight cast its glow, strong as laser beams, into the dining room.

Moonzy tugged at one of the laces on my high-tops with her teeth. "Um. Coral, you need to check this out."

I followed her over to an antique cabinet which took up the whole of the wall. Glass eyes stared out at us, wide and unblinking.

Tripping over my shoelace, I stumbled and knocked into the cabinet's door. A seagull swung backward and forward on a piece of string. Sitting on its back was a hedgehog wearing a flying helmet and a checked scarf that stuck out at right angles.

Underneath it, a badger, holding a withered bunch of flowers, shimmered ghost-like, in a coat made from dead cabbage white butterflies.

As I stepped back in horror, something in the bottom left-hand corner caught my eye. A Jack Russell dressed in coat-tails and a battered top hat, with a monocle and walking stick. I opened the cabinet gingerly and reached for its collar to find *Nip* engraved on the tag.

My rucksack dropped to the floor, hitting Moonzy, who squealed.

It was the same dog that had been on the missing poster at the bus stop.

"Who would do something as twisted as this?" Skaw fidgeted on my hat.

"Miss Mirk – she's the one who has been stealing the pets." I thought back to when I'd clocked her dragging a bin bag into her house in the middle of the night. It could easily have been full of stolen animals.

Moonzy's teeth rattled.

"I hope she's no' stuffed the wrecker bird – otherwise we're all stuffed." Skaw couldn't stop himself from trembling.

I paused, taking a deep breath. "Moonzy? Skaw? We'll have to keep our eyes peeled for God; no matter what has happened to him, I want him out of here."

"Of course," said Moonzy, nudging my foot.

"Goes without saying." Skaw wriggled into the fold of my hat. "Let's go. It pure gives me the dry boak in here."

The skull crunched over a carpet of dead flies to the door and poked her head out. "All clear!"

We left the room, listening for signs of Miss Mirk, but the house was quieter than clouds.

There were four doors leading off from the hallway, all of them closed. Moonzy jabbed her head in the direction of the one nearest to us.

I crossed over and gripped the handle. After counting to three, I turned it and swung the door open. The walls were plastered with missing pet posters, including the one I'd made for God.

I prayed we'd be in time to rescue all these poor creatures from Miss Mirk.

Moonzy, Skaw and I slunk down the hallway, checking every nook and cranny, calling out quietly for God and scouring the place for the wrecker bird. When we reached the last room, the door creaked as it opened.

Hundreds of cages were stacked on top of one another. Trapped birds trilled, cats arched their backs, dogs whined, a parrot flapped against the bars and a snake, with eyes like coin slots, flicked its tongue at me. Lizards froze, guinea pigs squeaked, goldfish darted behind algae-covered rocks and a tortoise hid its head in its shell.

I worked quickly, searching each and every one of the crates and tanks. Reaching the last row, panic began to rise in my chest. I couldn't spot God anywhere. Were we too late?

An almighty yowl came from a cage lying on its side on the floor. I hurried over to it and dropped to my knees. *Midnight Oasis Black* fur stuck out from between the thin metal bars. The cat's tail was short and stumpy.

"Godfrey!" I threw myself at the cage, sticking my fingers through the gaps to stroke him. He purred, his chest rattling like an old car engine.

Moonzy hurtled towards me, dodging a paw that flashed out of a cage to bat her. Skaw clung on to her eye socket for dear life.

"You found him!" she said.

"He's alive, Moonzy!" I grinned at her. "Any sign of the wrecker bird?"

"Nothing yet." Skaw hesitated and cocked his head, as if something had caught his attention.

The front door slammed shut and a light clicked on in the hallway.

We all stared at each other.

Skaw slipped through the bars of a hamster's cage and wiggled into a soggy pile of shredded newspaper. Moonzy dived into a fish tank, where a terrapin scrambled on top of her head. I glanced around; there was nowhere for me to hide.

I threw myself flat on the ground.

Miss Mirk strode along the corridor, the

floorboards creaking with every step. As she passed the doorway, God hurled himself against his cage, making it clatter.

The light above us blinked on. Miss Mirk entered the room, standing still, straining her ears for the same noise, which had attracted her attention in the first place. All the animals fell silent, sensing the impending danger.

The snake in the cage next to my face uncoiled and sped towards me.

Miss Mirk stepped forward. There was a rustling noise, as though she was digging through her handbag for something.

The snake lunged, snapping at my nose. I jerked my head back, smacking into a cage with a crow inside it, that cawed.

Miss Mirk put the light off and the door closed softly behind her.

I let my breath out and got to my feet as quietly as I could, not wanting to cause any more squawks, squeaks or growls.

Skaw popped up from the pile of paper; his eyes as large as marbles. As I frowned at him, a shadow flitted behind me. Before I could utter a sound, a cloth was pressed against my face. My head went woozy and the ground rushed up to meet me.

CHAPTER 15

I saw two pairs of slippers. I blinked and they merged into one pair. They were *Peony Tango* with furry pom-poms on them. One of them started tapping the ground – that's when I realized the pom-poms were rabbits' tails.

Miss Mirk elongated and then shrank. I rubbed my eyes.

"Word of advice: if you are going to break into someone's house, close the window after you sneak through it, otherwise it is a dead giveaway." Miss Mirk sat on a chair opposite me.

The stone floor was as cold as marble slabs. Junk and bric-a-brac were piled up everywhere. I tried to swallow, but my tongue felt as though it filled my entire mouth.

"You will be a little dopey – it is the chloroform. Makes the animals easier to handle, although I have to say, God put up an admirable fight. He gave me more scratches than a butcher's block when I caught him."

"You need help." It sounded as though my mouth was full of cotton wool. "I saw what was in your cabinet."

"Works of art, are they not? I have only just begun, but the plans I have in mind for the animals of Saltbay are quite spectacular!"

"What about all the kids who have lost their pets? They'll be heartbroken." A vein in my temple pulsed.

"If you love your animals, do not let them out of your sight, otherwise they can be here one minute and gone the next."

I sat up straight. "The wrecker bird wasn't a stray!"

"The wrecker whattie?" Miss Mirk pursed her lips.

"Beautiful bird: *Vintage Aubergine* chest, *Ebony King* eye mask, the most stunning *Electric Rainforest* tail feathers – you know, the ones in the hat you wore to my gran's funeral?"

"Is that what it is called? A wrecker bird? Well, I never," said Miss Mirk with a sniff. "It was on your cherry tree, singing its heart out, and I knew, that very second, I had to have it. Thought it must have escaped from a zoo or a private collection; its feathers are so exotic."

My heart used my ribcage as a trampoline. "Has it ended up in a cabinet too?"

"On the contrary, I have been busy designing a cropped feathered cape with matching trim for my gloves. I shall be the envy of everyone at the bingo."

I rested my head against the wall, relieved the wrecker bird was still very much alive. I concentrated hard on making my eyes focus. "Miss Mirk, I'm going to see you're put away for a very long time."

"Not necessarily." She pulled at her earlobe as she spoke. "Who knows you are here?"

My brain was so foggy, it was hard to think straight. "Nobody."

"Well, that is settled, then. You are going to have to stay in the cellar."

My mind clunked up a gear. "But that's kidnap!"

Miss Mirk's *Shark Skin* eyes hardened. "You broke into my house when I expressly warned you to stay away. You have left me with no other choice. You can stay hidden, until I have made my mind up what to do with you."

"Mum and Dad will be round searching for me!"

"They might, but it will be easy fobbing them off."

Miss Mirk was right. Mum and Dad had warned me to keep well away from her. They'd never in a million years guess I was here.

I gripped on to a metal filing cabinet to pull myself up. My legs buckled at the knees and I fell, sprawling out on the floor.

"Oh, Coral, you need to be much more careful. Can't have you coming to any harm now, can we?" Miss Mirk chuckled as she stood and grabbed me by the ankles. I attempted to shake her off, but I was too weak. As she hauled me over the ground, I grasped on to a chair, holding on for dear life. Miss Mirk let go of my feet and my limbs thudded to the floor. She prised my fingers off the wood, one by one. "Behave yourself and I'll feed you soup, once a day." She leaned in closer. "Disobey me, Coral, and who knows? You might end up in a cabinet yourself." Her eyes glittered behind her glasses.

Fear tensed every muscle in my body; I stopped struggling.

Miss Mirk hefted me over to a trapdoor in the floor, which she flung open, before finding some old bedding and pillows to chuck down into it. She then laid me out, at the edge of the hole. I peered into a chasm as dark as nightmares. I thought about Lyart being held hostage by Muckle Red. I hoped, with all my heart, he was safe.

As Miss Mirk prepared to roll me in, there was a scratching noise at the door.

Her minuscule eyes found mine.

There it was again.

Miss Mirk tutted. "It will be that jackdaw – he is forever unpicking the lock on his cage. Far too clever for his own good if you ask me. I should wring his neck." She adjusted her glasses and walked over to the door, flinging it open.

The scream was the loudest noise I'd ever heard Miss Mirk make.

Standing in the doorway was a *Paprika Sprinkle* cat with *Jungle Tigress* stripes. As it shuffled forward, sawdust spilled out from its sides. It raised its tail and gazed at Miss Mirk, its eyes *Sulphur Yellow*.

"*George?* Is that really you?" Miss Mirk's hand fluttered up to her chest. "But I thought you had left me for pet heaven? How can this be?" She removed her spectacles and pinched the bridge of her nose, as though trying to make sense of it all.

This must have been the *George* Miss Mirk had mentioned at Gran's funeral – the same *George* the vet had put down. It was plain to see she had attempted to preserve the cat, but how on earth had it come back to life?

George meowed and Miss Mirk stepped back from him, warily. "I have angered you. That is why you have returned."

The cat gave a yowl.

"I knew it! It is because of the other pets in the house? Please do not be jealous – they mean nothing to me. They are never allowed up on the settee or my bed, like you were."

The cat's tail puffed up and its ears twitched.

Miss Mirk stumbled away from it. "I only ever hand-fed you sardines from the tin or poured organic cream into your saucer."

George advanced towards her, as if he was stalking a mouse.

Glancing at the door, I saw my chance to escape. I wobbled to my feet just as an *Ashes of Roses* worm wriggled into the room.

My eyes flicked over to Miss Mirk, who slowly raised her hands up as if to calm the cat. "A-and I would never ever let any of them wear your jumper. Remember the one I knitted for you with the robin on it? How you used to love hunting them in the garden."

The cat twitched its tail in annoyance, completely ignoring me and Skaw.

That's when it dawned on me: the cat hadn't come back to life – Moonzy had left the skull and changed into it to distract Miss Mirk!

George hissed at Miss Mirk, who, desperate to

escape from him, turned and fled, forgetting the trapdoor was still open.

Miss Mirk fell into the cellar, yelling all the way down, until she hit the bedding, where she muttered some words I never thought I'd hear an elderly lady say.

I staggered over to the trapdoor. Miss Mirk was lucky the only thing she had broken was her glasses.

"I ought to have buried George in the herbaceous border while I had the chance. I do not know what trickery you have just played on me, but get me out this instant!" she spluttered.

"Miss Mirk, here's a little taster of what life will be like for you, because you're going to be put away for a very long time," I replied.

She narrowed her eyes at me. "If you leave me, I'll come for that ugly cat of yours when you least expect it and..." I slammed the trapdoor shut, not wanting to listen to another word. "I can't thank the pair of you enough for what you've done. Moonzy, how did you know George was her cat?"

"She'd put a name plaque on a small display cabinet upstairs and none of the others had one, so we figured he had been special to her – and would give her a bit of a scare if he came back to life." Moonzy stretched and then licked her paw.

"We've still no' found the wrecker bird, Coral." Skaw shook his head.

"The bird is alive, Skaw. It's got to be in this house, somewhere!"

The worm's eyes lit up and he stood straight. Moonzy raised her ears and some whiskers fell off.

"You need to change back into the skull, otherwise you'll never make it to the graveyard in one piece," said Skaw.

"Good point. I'll be two minutes." Moonzy tottered over to the door.

Skaw paused. "We let God out, Coral. We thought he'd have no problem finding his way home."

"Thank you, Skaw. We can deal with the others tomorrow – at least they'll be safe from Miss Mirk tonight." I picked Skaw up, placing him on my shoulder. I looked at my watch and sighed: I'd missed my curfew. Mum and Dad would be furious and if they got in touch with Isla, they'd know I'd been lying to them about where I was.

"Come on, Coral – there's only one room left on the second floor to search."

I pushed my worries about Mum and Dad to the back of my mind and hurried out to the stairs, climbing them two at a time.

As the top landing came into view, Skaw's voice filled with excitement. "It's the one at the end!"

I hared along the corridor, shoved the door open and raced inside. The walls of the bedroom were adorned in *Hot Peach Flesh* flowery wallpaper. There were piles of clothes, newspapers, boxes and toy animals everywhere. I put Skaw down on the bed as Moonzy rolled through the doorway behind us. The skull sprang on to the mattress and bounced around to get a better view of the room.

"On top of the wardrobe?" Skaw suggested.

I knocked down some hat boxes. Money-off coupons spilled out from them, falling to the floor the same way as ticker tape in a parade.

"Coral!" Moonzy hollered. "By the window!"

Poking out from the bottom of the full-length curtains were the feet of a metal stand. I clambered over boxes to pull back the curtain. Behind them was an object covered in a shawl. In one sweeping move, I whipped it off. There, inside a *Distant Star Silver* cage, was a bird with a plump *Vintage Aubergine* chest and a clump of long every-colour-of-green tail feathers, that shone *Evergreen Neon* in the rays of the Hallow moon.

The wrecker bird's head tilted towards me; its eyes flashed as it blinked. It started to sing and a rainbow of light beams burst out from its beak, lighting up the room with glorious waves of colour. The bird's tune was so beautiful, my heart soared with joy. The same way it had when I'd been in the church with Gran, listening to the choir and marvelling at the stained-glass windows.

A creature as precious as the wrecker bird didn't belong in a cage.

I clicked open the latch and there was a whisper of air against my skin as it brushed past me and sailed out the door.

"No, Coral!" cried Moonzy.

The light trails behind it fell to the floor in a shower of sparkles and my heart ached as it left. All my sad thoughts came flooding back to me and I sagged under the weight of them.

Moonzy picked Skaw up between her teeth and thudded to the floor in hot pursuit of the bird.

What had I been thinking?

Useless, stupid girl. You can't even capture a bird in a cage.

My thoughts hurt more than cuts. I had to put this right.

Shooting out of the bedroom, I tore down the stairs, following the sound of Skaw's yells.

"Moonzy!" shouted the worm. "*What are you doing?*"

Moonzy was on the dining room table, dangling Skaw between her jaws as if he was bait on a hook. "Here, birdie, birdie, birdie," she said through clenched teeth.

The creatures in the cabinet watched on, silently.

A movement by the window caught my eye.

The net curtains billowed in the breeze, framing a small silhouette with a crown of feathers on its head. The wrecker bird hopped forward, sticking its beak through the window. If it escaped into the night, it would be lost to us, for ever.

Skaw's eyes were filled with terror. "Moonzy, I'm begging you."

"I'll do anything to find Lyart. I can't lose this bird, Skaw, and I don't care what I've got to do to get it." Moonzy waggled the worm. "Here, birdie, birdie. Come and get the juicy worm."

The wrecker bird bobbed up and down, and then swooped towards them, skidding over the surface of the table, the same way ducks land on ice. It snatched Skaw out from between Moonzy's teeth and swallowed him whole.

"Rucksack. Now, Coral!" Moonzy roared at me.

I snatched the bag up from the floor and ripped it open. Before the wrecker bird could move a feather, I seized it and shoved it under my arm, pinning its wings to its sides.

"Sorry about this." I forced my fingers into its beak and tickled its throat. The bird coughed, its chest heaving as it regurgitated Skaw out on to the table. I whisked the wrecker bird into the bag, rainbows strobing out from the top of the rucksack until I zipped it firmly shut.

Skaw lay still, covered in clear slime. I cleaned his

face and rubbed his back. The worm hiccupped, his *Ashes of Roses* colour slowly returning.

"What did you go and do that for?" The skull stuck her jaw out.

"He's saved my life twice now, Moonzy."

The skull threw me a look darker than cellars.

"Skaw, do you know where Lyart is?" He went to open his mouth but thought better of it. He shook his head.

"Moonzy, if we don't leave this minute, we'll miss the Hallow moon and if that happens, we'll never discover where Lyart is hidden because Muckle Red will take the secret to his grave with him when he perishes."

The skull clacked her teeth but didn't say another word.

I slipped Skaw into my hat and lifted Moonzy up. As I crawled back out through the window, the whole of Saltbay blanched *Swan Wing* in the last of the light from the Hallow moon.

CHAPTER
16

Tendrils of mist wrapped themselves around the gravestones and the Hallow moonlight pushed past the branches to illuminate all the statues and cherubs *Lightning Flash*.

"The one time you actually want Muckle Red to show up and he's nowhere to be seen." I booted a conker away in frustration.

"I'll go and find the heart-stealing, no-good, rotten, lopsided maniac." Moonzy jumped down from the rucksack.

"You won't find anyone matching that description here," the worm called after her.

I plucked Skaw from my hat. "You OK?"

"Never better." His face was scrunched up in pain. "Coral? Muckle Red will be in the tunnels. As soon as you enter them, he'll know you're here."

"Thanks, Skaw." I peered at my watch: we'd not long to go until the Hallow moon left for good. My pulse beat to the same time as an out-of-control metronome.

I jogged over to the headstone with the engravings on it, and pressed them in the same order Lyart had done. The stairs opened up in the ground.

"Moonzy!" I yelled. "Over here!"

Skaw writhed in my hand. "One more thing, Coral: I don't know what Muckle Red has done with Lyart as they were outside his chamber in the corridor, but I do remember seeing a bright flash of green-and-yellow light."

"Why are you telling me this?"

"If it hadn't been for you, I'd still be inside the wrecker bird." Skaw sighed. "And I know how much you want to be with your gran again."

I placed Skaw on my shoulder. "I learned in biology that worms have five hearts. You've got it in you to be five times braver, kinder and more loving than any of us – if you wish."

His *Slate in the Rain* eyes lit up and then darkened as Moonzy approached.

"Wait for me!" The skull crashed through the grass towards us.

I hated that we had to go back underground. As we descended deeper into the tunnels, it was hard not to shiver. There was something about the place which got under my skin and set my nerves on edge. I pushed the fear to the back of my mind and mulled over the green-and-yellow flash Skaw had mentioned, but it made no sense. Nothing in here was that colour.

Arriving at the burial chamber of Lyart's family, I placed Skaw in an alcove as far away from Moonzy as possible. I peeked into the rucksack, checking the bird was OK and the witch's tears were safe. "Moonzy – we need to think fast; where can we hide the witch's tears and wrecker bird so Muckle Red won't find them?"

The skull's jaw fell open. "You're not seriously wanting to discuss something as important as this with that worm listening in?"

I eyed Skaw. "He won't say a word."

Moonzy flared her nasal cavities. "Are you really going to trust him when there's so much at stake? Have you forgotten he's best pals with a psychopath?"

Skaw poked his head over the side of the alcove. "You've attempted to bump me off twice now. You're the one with the problem!"

"Come over here and say that to my face!" Moonzy flushed *Scottish Heather*.

The noise of rushing air silenced us all. Without warning, bones burst through the earth and a skull somersaulted out of the wall, landing on top of a rickety pile of vertebrae. *Oxblood* hair exploded from his scalp and a patch snapped over his left eye. With a final clack of leg bones, Muckle Red shuddered to life. "Your expression, Coral Glen! A picture of all things unsightly."

I flicked my eyes over to Moonzy and the rucksack. Everything needed to break the spell was within his reach.

Moonzy sneaked behind a fallen picture frame. If she stayed still, Muckle Red might not notice she was there.

Skaw drew himself to his full height in the alcove.

The Heart Collector squinted at him. "Skaw! You're cutting it narrow? Leaving it till the last gasp. I must be free before the Hallow moon wanes."

The worm cleared his throat. "Do you no' mean *we* must be free?"

Muckle Red dismissed Skaw with an overdramatic eye roll.

Skaw set his mouth in a line. "If it wasn't for me, you wouldn't have everything you need to break the spell."

Muckle Red stormed over to the worm in a flurry of cracks. "You got all the objects, including a real, live wrecker bird?"

Skaw's eyes glinted as the moonlight does on barbed wire. "The wrecker bird and witch's tears are in the rucksack."

I sucked my breath in. If Skaw gave away Moonzy's hiding place, Muckle Red would be able to leave Halloway.

"What about the cannibal bones?" growled

Muckle Red.

Skaw avoided my gaze. "You'll find one of Sully Tarn's victim's skulls behind that picture, over there. Watch out, it's inhabited by an evil poltergeist."

My heart sank all the way down into the soles of my high-tops. Moonzy had been right not to trust Skaw. The worm had said from the very start he'd not betray Muckle Red; I'd been foolish enough to think otherwise.

Muckle Red swooped on the rucksack. As he lifted up the picture, Moonzy shot forward as fast as bullets to bite his hand. Muckle Red whacked the skull with so much force her jaw fell off. Before she could move, he gathered her up and stuffed her inside the rucksack. The Heart Collector snatched Skaw from the alcove. "The north star can't dazzle as you do, worm." His words fell as icicles to the ground.

Anger coursed through my veins, thawing the chill on my skin. I pounced forward on to Muckle Red's back, striking him with my fists.

The Heart Collector vanished into thin air beneath me; his bones and I tumbled to the ground.

I landed awkwardly on jagged ribs and groaned.

Muckle Red had gone without telling me where Lyart was.

Why had I not hidden the rucksack and Moonzy somewhere in the tunnels? Then I could have haggled for Lyart's safe release.

I was alone, with no idea where Lyart was. I'd not only lost Skaw and Moonzy, but I'd thrown away my chance to tell Gran I loved her: the one thing that had been keeping me going. And even worse, Muckle Red had everything he needed to escape and steal children's hearts.

I stumbled into the corridor, the walls closing in on me. I fell to my knees, coughing, willing myself to take a gulp of air. Straight above, the glow from a *Breath of Spring*–coloured glamp was so luminous, it hurt my eyes.

I took some slow and steady breaths.

Moonzy's life might be in grave danger now that Muckle Red had her.

Frustrated, I yanked at some tree roots poking out from the wall and noticed my hand was bathed in the *Breath of Spring* glow. It came back to me how Moonzy had described Lyart's aura as the purest green imaginable.

I crawled over to the glamp. Skaw had said he'd spotted a green-and-yellow flash when Lyart had vanished. I thought about the paint charts on my walls – the small rectangle of *Breath of Spring* was green, except there was a hint of yellow in it too.

I leapt to my feet and looked along the row of glamps. There wasn't another the same colour as this one. I tapped the side of it to see if a face would appear, but nothing happened.

What if I broke it and it was full of negative energy?

It was a risk I was going to have to take. I pulled my scarf over my nose, picked up the glamp and threw it against the wall. The glass exploded and the light whizzed out, denting the walls and making earth rain down from the ceiling.

As it zoomed towards me, I ducked, covering my head with my arms.

I heard the sound of something heavy landing next to me and opened one eye.

"Thanks for getting me out of there." Lyart stood, shaking out his arms and legs.

"Lyart!" I gave him a hug. "I've made a mess of everything; Muckle Red has the witch's tears, cannibal bones and the wrecker bird." I paused. "He took Moonzy too; she's in the skull we stole from the cannibal. I'm so sorry."

Lyart touched the side of my arm. "She's more than capable of holding her own, but I think it's high time we put a stop to Muckle Red. Ready?"

I sniffed and nodded.

The glamps flickered as we dashed along the passageway, hurdling over mossy stones and bursting through dust-clad curtains of tree roots.

"Where are we going?" I panted.

"Muckle Red needs the Hallow moon to break the spell. There's only one place where its light can appear underground." After what seemed like ages, Lyart slowed and halted by an archway. Chiselled into the stone above was: *The Passage of Lost Souls*.

"Coral, the quickest way for us to reach Muckle Red is through here."

I gazed into the tunnel. Goosebumps crept over my flesh.

"The souls thrive off negative energy, so keep

264

your thoughts clear of anything upsetting and whatever you do, don't stop for anyone – just remember nothing is real. Can you do that?"

I thought about Moonzy being at the mercy of Muckle Red. "Yes."

"You go first. Hurry!"

Stepping inside the tunnel, I noticed the air was damp.

I glanced back at Lyart, who gave me a reassuring smile.

There were no glamps or glow-worms to light the way. I strode forward, ignoring the fear sitting barrel-heavy in the pit of my stomach.

If I had ever been scared of the dark, Gran would tell me the night-time was nothing to be afraid of, because the world needed its rest as well.

A figure appeared further ahead, glowing softly like a night light. I pretended it wasn't there, concentrating hard on putting one foot in front of the other.

As I passed it, the figure followed me, its stride matching mine. I quickened the pace and it sped up too.

"You're walking as fast as God does when he

knows there's turkey in his bowl."

I stifled a sob, hearing her voice again.

It took every bit of strength I had not to look at her.

She wasn't real. This was a trick.

"How has your day been, Coral?" she asked.

Those were the words I missed the most. The same words she'd never say to me again.

I couldn't help myself.

Gran rewarded me with her smile – the one she always gave me when I came home from school. I must have imagined this moment a million times or more since she'd left us.

I cleared my throat. "*Sunshiny Days*, Gran."

"That's a cheery colour?" Gran fiddled with her earring.

I hated myself for already forgetting she did that. "It's how I feel because you're here. . . I've missed you terribly." My voice was barely a whisper.

"Are you sure, Coral? It's your fault I'm dead."

I pressed the back of my hand over my mouth. The weight inside me grew heavier than mountains. Putting my head down, I walked on.

"Thought *Killer Khaki* or *Murdering Mauve* might be more appropriate, considering," she hissed, her words dancing around me in echoes.

"You left me!" she shrieked.

I clapped my hands over my ears and sprinted forward.

I couldn't breathe.

I had to get out of here.

Spying a glimmer of light up ahead, I tore towards it, throwing myself out the other side, like an athlete over the finishing line.

All you do is cause death and misery.

I wanted to see the stars again – to take the night air into my lungs.

Lyart shot out of the tunnel moments later, his breaths fast and shallow. "The place never gets any easier."

I walked away from him.

"Coral?" He caught up with me. "What happened in there came from your own thoughts. None of it was real."

"Even so, everything I do goes wrong and now Moonzy could be in danger because of me."

Lyart frowned, his freckles bunching together. "All I see is a brave girl who has put her life on the line for the opportunity be with her gran again. If we can destroy Muckle Red, I will honour my word and take you to her, but we don't have much time left."

I tilted my head back, taking in our surroundings. "Where is this?"

"An abandoned copper mine."

The moonlight stretched down through holes in the roof to shimmer on the *Phoenix Tears* lake. Wavy-lined reflections rose and fell, like monitored heartbeats, on the *Lost Ark Gold*–coloured walls. Thousands of moths gathered over the lake's surface, moving together in a vast cloud, their *Moon Mist* wings whispering as they beat.

Flakes of snow gently drifted past us; I buttoned my coat up. Strewn all over the place were discarded pieces of rusted machinery and wires.

Lyart pointed towards the water. "There's something on the shore."

We picked our way over the stones to find an ancient coffin. The lid was askew and it was empty inside.

"Who do you think this belonged to?" I asked, noticing all the deep scratches in the wood.

"It's mine," said a voice behind me.

Lyart and I nearly jumped out of our skins.

"I've forever waited to be rid of it." Muckle Red smirked.

Lyart hastened towards him, clenching his fists. "What have you done with Moonzy?"

Skaw wiggled on to Muckle Red's shoulder. "She did her usual and vanished when the going got tough. She'll probably be a slug or a bit of grit by now."

Relief washed through me that Moonzy had escaped.

The Heart Collector reached into the stolen rucksack for the witch's tears and placed the pot into the coffin. Next, he dropped in the skull, which clattered as it rolled along the base of it.

He was reversing the spell that had kept him trapped in the graveyard!

Lastly, he produced the wrecker bird, which had been bound with rope. Its crown of feathers drooped and its eyes had dulled. Muckle Red flung it inside the coffin, pounding the lid shut with his fist, so everything was sealed in.

The moonlight glazed the surface of the wood. My throat ached as the bird thumped against the sides of it, trying to get out.

The ground shuddered and giant *Night Swim* waves reared up. The lake whirled and gurgled as it drained away, revealing a *Cloak of Mystery*–coloured doorway. Floundering fish flashed *Polished Pebble*, as they sought out the last remaining puddles of water.

Muckle Red's body creaked and popped one last time as he became solid flesh and bone in front of our eyes. When he stretched, his muscles filled out and his dusty heart darkened to once again beat in his chest.

The spell was finally broken; the Heart Collector was ready to leave the graveyard.

I flicked my eyes at my watch; only minutes to go before the Hallow moon vanished for good.

Muckle Red strode towards the doorway, Skaw proudly perched on his shoulder.

"There's something I need to know!" I shouted after them, praying Muckle Red would stop.

The Heart Collector checked the moonlight was still piercing through the holes in the ceiling. "Make it electricity-quick; I have children to hunt." He adjusted the chain of dripping hearts around his neck.

"Aye, very funny. You nearly had me going there," hooted Skaw, nudging Muckle Red with his head.

I approached warily, cricking my neck up at him. "Why did you want the witches to take the blame for what you did?"

Lyart joined me, standing by my side.

Muckle Red's arctic-cold breath whistled through his teeth. "Seeing as how I'm on the cusp of wildness and freedom, I'll indulge you. Black Belly Fever swept through Saltbay; my father coughed blood and a cross was slapped on our door. The doctor refused to take any notice because we were penniless and all my begging and pleas in the town for help went ignored. I'd heard whispers of a witch and her potent potions, so I searched high and low for her." Muckle Red's eye flickered and his nostrils narrowed. "Septic brains, gangrenous boils, death by scratching; Carline Deedclathes didn't cure, she killed. *Disease is nature's way of getting rid of vermin*, she said. I was sent packing with empty hands and scorn-filled ears. After my father's last rattling breath, I plotted and planned the downfall of her and all those others responsible for his death. Black magic was a far greater fear than Black Belly Fever. All it took was the stealing of children's hearts for everyone to blame, hunt and torch the hags into ash piles." Muckle Red shrugged. "Revenge was sweetness."

"Hang on!" interrupted Skaw. "Let's just rewind here a second. You're no' being serious, are you?" The worm gawped at Muckle Red.

"You don't half pick moments of the worst possible, Skaw. Get lost."

The worm peered closely into Muckle Red's eye. "But you've worked so hard to put the past behind you – don't ruin it all now."

"Skaw!" Muckle Red said it in a way that indicated the worm should know better. "The spell has denied me the chance to add hearts to my collection for two hundred years. I'm not waiting any longer."

Skaw nodded his head as if he'd made his mind

up about something. "If you really want a new heart – take one of mine. I'd do anything for my best mate, especially if it halts your desire to kill until we can get you the help you need to cure you of this terrible affliction for once and for all."

The Heart Collector wheezed with laughter, a *Salty Peat* drip leaking from his eye. "A gritty little worm ticker next to these magnificent specimens? Your heart will be so puny, it wouldn't be worth the bother."

It took Skaw a second or two for Muckle Red's words to sink in. "I told everyone you'd changed!" The worm glared at him. "Except you've no', have you? I cannae believe I fell for that rot you spouted about being sorry for what you'd done in the past. Moonzy had you sussed the whole time, and the worst thing is, I refused to listen to her – no wonder she hates my guts."

Muckle Red gritted his teeth. "You are a fool much gullible. You forever bored me rigid and would never have been my companion on the world adventures."

"You used me!" Skaw's eyes filled up and his

cheeks flushed *Cabernet Cork*. The worm puffed his chest out. "I've got five hearts and that's way more bravery, kindness and love than you'll ever know, Muckle Red."

The Heart Collector's face stretched into a smile. "Enjoy your trip, worm." He plucked Skaw off his shoulder and hurled him away with force. Skaw zipped through the air, thwacked into the side of the coffin and dropped from view.

My heartbeat tripled and anger turned every cell in my body *White Hot*. "How Skaw never saw through you is a complete mystery! If you've hurt him in any way I'm going to . . ."

Muckle Red towered over me. "The worm's heart is useless – but yours is twinned in feistiness with my own, Coral Glen, and I must have it," he said, patting his chain. "Think of it as a farewell gift from you to me."

A fear as cold as the depths of winter stole through my veins.

"You're not laying a finger on her." Lyart squared up to Muckle Red, his eyes blazing.

Muckle Red opened his mouth, blasting Lyart

with his subzero breath. Lyart raised his arms to shield himself, but it was too late; his entire body became encased in *Wind Chill Blue* ice.

The Heart Collector gave him a shove.

If Lyart fell on the stones, he'd shatter into a million pieces!

I scrambled forward, catching Lyart in the nick of time, and gently lowered him to the ground.

Something whistled overhead and Muckle Red teetered back, the full force of the rock hitting him like a cannonball.

A girl with *Copper Still* ringlets skidded to a halt, her *Mythical Nights* dress swishing around her. Clutched in her hand was another stone at the ready. "You don't have a heart, Muckle Red, that's why you steal other people's," she shouted.

Muckle Red snorted. "Hearts are made to be broken."

"Coral's is one you'll never own." Her *Pomegranate Seed* lips were thin lines across her *Seagull Belly* skin.

There was only one girl I knew as courageous as this.

The Heart Collector slammed into Moonzy,

sending her flying. In one swift move, he pinned her to the ground.

I saw the look in his eye. If I didn't do something fast, he would finish her off.

Just past Moonzy was Muckle Red's coffin. He was supposed to perish on the night of the Hallow moon, not us. That's when it struck me – if I could release the wrecker bird from its wooden prison, the spell would be broken.

"Coral!" Moonzy squealed. "I can't change into anything else – I've chosen to be me from now on; the timing . . . couldn't . . . have . . . been worse."

As Muckle Red tightened his grip on her, the hearts he wore around his neck trembled. Moonzy's *Celestial Spark* glow began to flicker and fade.

If I didn't do something, Muckle Red would destroy her for good.

Pelting towards the coffin, my fingers scrabbled around the edge of the lid to lift it, but it was wedged shut. Picking up a rock, I smashed it down on the wood, praying it would crack.

Hearing a gasp from Moonzy, I spun around.

Her eyes widened and her whole body shuddered

before she went limp. The Heart Collector finally let go of her and advanced towards me.

"No!" I yelled at the top of my voice.

"It's over, Coral Glen." Muckle Red grabbed me and held the palm of his hand over my heart. My spine curved as I felt it being pulled, as though Muckle Red was somehow coaxing it out of my body.

I twisted from side to side, trying to fight him off, until I caught sight of Moonzy lying still and lifeless. It wouldn't have been possible to collect all the objects without her help. And the thought of never being able to talk to my friend again hurt so badly, it was as though my insides were filled with cut glass.

A crushing sadness tore through me; tears streamed down my cheeks.

Lyart would be devastated that Moonzy had been taken from us.

My heart broke all over again.

Muckle Red sensed me weakening and licked his lips.

The wrecker bird started thumping hard against the coffin until it splintered. A hole appeared and the bird poked its head out. Before Muckle Red could slam his hand down over it, the bird burst through the lid and corkscrewed into the darkness above. The song that filled the copper mine was so exquisite, Muckle Red let go of me to cover his ears, as if in pain. Falling to the ground, I shuffled away from him.

The wrecker bird returned to sweep low over the lakebed, changing the puddles into liquid rainbows. It sang and the moths parted to gather around every hole in the roof, blocking out the moonlight.

With the bird free from the coffin and the moonlight gone, the spell had been reversed. Realizing he could never leave the graveyard now, Muckle Red sprang towards me, his teeth bared. The second before he reached me, he exploded into a million sparks of *Planet Fever*, with the ferocity of a firework. The last of his curses bounced off the rocks and faded into nothingness.

The moths scattered and the wrecker bird vanished through the ceiling, leaving behind a falling trail of every-colour-under-the-sun glitter.

Lyart knelt next to me, water dripping from him.

The ice must have melted when Muckle Red was destroyed!

My hand grabbed his arm. "It's Moonzy. There was nothing I could do."

His *Secret Garden Ivy* eyes clouded and his head swivelled to see where she was lying. To both of our astonishment, Moonzy's fingers twitched.

Lyart helped me to my feet and, together, we hurried to her side. She opened her eyes. "I remembered *The Mythical Birds of the World* book, Coral. The wrecker bird shows up to bring comfort to those in grief. I knew if you thought I was no longer alive, you'd be distraught, and that the bird would do everything to get out, so it could make you feel better. It's because of your tears that it left the coffin and broke the spell, Coral."

I stared at her in wonder. Moonzy was about the smartest person I'd ever known. "You gave me a terrible scare. Please, never do that again." I hugged her tight, even though it made her wince.

Lyart checked his pocket watch. "Coral, we only have a couple of minutes left before midnight."

"Go, while there is still time." Moonzy smiled at me.

Lyart snatched my hand and the cavern whirled around us. I screamed as my body was shaken to its core.

CHAPTER
17

Above me, the shapes of trees were outlined by the stars, arranged in intricate patterns. The air was clear and sweet; I gulped it in, not sure if I was asleep or awake.

"Coral?" Lyart pulled me to my feet and saw the quizzical expression on my face. "You've just experienced speed-of-light travel, courtesy of the fact I'm a ghost," he explained as he broke into a sprint. "We don't have a zeptosecond to lose!"

We ran between trees so tall, planets spun on the tips of them.

I wasn't sure if I was imagining it, but I thought I spied *Dusky Parakeet* sparkles every time I moved. "Where are we?"

"The bridge between earth and heaven." Lyart gazed at the horizon beyond the trees, which stretched out in the longest line I'd ever seen.

"I thought you couldn't leave the graveyard?"

"I can't – this place is connected to it. Come on!"

We slipped down a bank, soft *Buttered Corn* sand cushioning our feet. At the bottom, we crouched behind some dune grass, dewdrops hanging from its blades like Christmas baubles.

A *Deep Secret* ocean sighed in front of us, its foam-tipped waves whispering on to the sand, teasing the land with its presence, before rushing away again.

The Hallow moon hung low, the last of its rays touching the figures gathered on the shore. One by one, they waded into the sea, *Golden Nectar* beams strobing out from their bodies until they became small globes filled with the light of a thousand moons. Set loose from the bonds of the earth, they flickered and rose playfully, the same way as sparks do from a fire, until they joined the stars, where it was hard to tell one from the other.

"I'm too late!" I held my breath, scanning the shore until finally I spotted her, wading into the water. Every emotion of hurt, guilt, rage, pain, loss and bewilderment I'd felt since Gran had left us returned, making my heart squeeze and flutter, and my limbs heavy.

"Her crossing has started," said Lyart.

"Oh, Lyart. No, no, no. . ." Tears clouded my eyes as I sprang up. I wiped them away frantically, never wanting to lose sight of her again. I tore across the tide-flattened sand, weaving my way between the other souls.

I called her name as I reached the waves. Long flashes of *Golden Nectar* light flared out from Gran's body. I waded through the water towards her, a heartbeat away from telling her how sorry I was for what had happened and how much I loved her. As I stretched out my arms, she became a ball of light and danced around in the air, just beyond the reach of my fingertips. She climbed up, illuminating the whole sky *Stardust Highway*. I caught the scent of geranium and rose on the wind. My tears blinded me as I lost her to the heavens.

The sweet breath of the sea was replaced by the scent of chilled stone, damp leaves and freshly dug earth.

My eyes burned and my throat hurt. "Why did you bring me back to Halloway?"

"That place is not for those who still have their lives to live here," he answered.

I pressed the palms of my hands into my eyes. I could no longer hold everything in. "I left her all alone, Lyart. She'd asked me to tidy my room and I sneaked out to meet a friend." I dropped my hands to my sides. "If I'd stayed at home, none of this would have happened. I would have known she wasn't well and saved her, and she wouldn't be a trillion miles away." I glared up at the *Wrought Iron* sky, the anger in my eyes flashing brighter than the stars. "She always put me first and the one time she needed me, I wasn't even there. What if she had been calling me for help? Or if it was me going off without saying a word that made her ill in the first place? How can I live the rest of my life with this going round and round in my head, every second of every day?" My voice cracked like a dropped mirror. "She must have been so disappointed in me for what I did. I know I am."

"There's something I want to show you, Coral." Lyart rolled up his sleeves.

I stood, trembling and raw, as if the top layer of my skin had been peeled away, exposing all my nerve endings.

Raising my eyes, I noticed a crowd of children had gathered beside Gran's grave.

I stepped away in fright.

Lyart smiled. "It's OK, Coral. They're here because they want to thank you."

"Why?"

"Their hearts were released to them when Muckle Red perished." Lyart placed both hands on the top of Gran's headstone.

The children whispered and shuffled closer together, linking arms. A *Deep Universe* cloud formed above their heads. As it lit up, images flickered to life as though a film was being played.

I could see a woman with *Pain au Chocolat* hair,

in a hospital bed, holding a baby wrapped in a *Cottage Rose* blanket. A man was seated next to her. He picked up the baby and cradled it, kissing its head. The woman smiled and reached out to stroke the baby's cheek.

I blinked.

It was Mum and Dad; not as they were now but when they were younger.

Was the baby me?

The image swirled and broke up as the cloud darkened. I was about to ask Lyart what this was, when the cloud illuminated once again. This time, I saw the sun dancing on water in flares and sparkles. A girl was standing at the end of a wooden jetty. I recognized my swimsuit with the *Bashful Pink* flamingos on it. I leapt off the pier into the loch. Seconds later, my head broke through the surface and I pulled off my goggles as I whooped and splashed around.

It was me at Loch Tay!

I smiled at seeing myself so happy and carefree.

Lyart's eyes were closed in concentration.

What was this?

I appeared in the mist again, this time sitting cross-legged under a sign that said: *Please do not eat in the library*. I had a large storybook balanced on my lap and Tatty the squirrel was tucked under my arm. I was busy jabbing my finger at the pictures, completely unaware I was being watched.

The cloud above the earthbound filled with the familiar colours of Saltbay beach. My curls lifted in the wind and my cheeks were flushed *Wild Morello Cherry*. "I love you, Gran," I mouthed, before running over the sand to chase a swallow, ice cream clutched in my hand.

The mist burst into a kaleidoscope of reds, yellows, blues, greens and purples. Stained-glass windows emerged from the fog and the choir sang their hearts out. My eyes shone candlelight-bright as I beamed at Gran and snuggled into her.

When the church faded, the clouds began to dissolve, vanishing into the sky.

The children stepped away, melting into the trees in the background.

Lyart let go of the headstone and straightened up.

Tears streaked down my face, luminous with the radiance of stars.

Moonzy hurried over to give me a hug. "Those

were your gran's last thoughts before she passed away."

Goosebumps rose on my arms, my skin alive with tingles.

Lyart tugged his sleeves back down. "Coral, when loved ones leave us, their minds are never filled with pain, hate or fear, but with the things that brought them the greatest happiness in their lives."

My eyes welled up again; the graveyard rippled as though in a heatwave.

"I swear, I'd do anything for someone to heart me that much," said a familiar voice.

"Skaw!" I sniffed, wiping my nose. "You're OK!"

The worm was perched on Moonzy's shoulder, dabbing at his eyes. "These are no' tears, by the way. The cold's nipping them."

"Would you believe I found him inside Muckle Red's coffin before I left?" said Moonzy. "It was Skaw who'd gnawed through the ropes around the wrecker bird, which meant it could escape. I thought that was pretty brave of him considering the bird almost ate him for dinner. Couldn't leave him behind after that."

Skaw gazed adoringly at Moonzy.

"I loved you as Tatty the squirrel – but it's wonderful to finally see the real you!" I said to her.

Moonzy laughed, flushing *Piggy Bank*.

I faced Lyart. "I don't know how I can ever thank you for showing me Gran's memories."

"You've kept a world of children safe from Muckle Red – your thanks aren't needed," said Lyart.

"You've got a gob on you and anger-management issues, but you're one of the bravest lassies I've ever met," piped up Skaw.

Moonzy prodded him with her finger.

"Make that two of the angriest, gobbiest, most courageous lassies I've ever met," he said.

Moonzy grinned. "I think you and me might just get along after all, Skaw."

The worm dropped his head as though he was thinking about how to word something that wasn't going to be easy to say. "I'm so sorry I never believed you about Muckle Red." He bit his lip. "Would it be OK if I stayed to help keep the graveyard safe? It's the only way I can think of to make up for everything and besides, there's nowhere else on the planet I'd rather be."

Lyart glanced from Moonzy to Skaw. "How would you two like to join me in becoming Keepers of Halloway? I think you've both proved yourselves more than worthy of the job."

Moonzy let out a squeal and leapt forward to hug Lyart.

Skaw flattened himself against her neck to avoid being crushed, his *Slate in the Rain* eyes watering again. "Nothing would make me prouder."

The gate to the graveyard squeaked open; we stared at one another as footsteps raced up the path.

"Coral!" shouted Dad.

"Are you here?" Mum's voice was thin with fear.

Moonzy gasped. "You never made it home after Miss Mirk's house. They'll think something awful has happened to you."

I walked slowly out from behind Gran's gravestone. I'd survived Carline Deedclathes, Sully Tarn, Miss Mirk and Muckle Red, only to be killed by my parents for disappearing off without telling them where I was going.

I took a really deep breath. As I braced myself, I

noticed the heavy weight inside me had gone, and I knew I could deal with whatever Mum and Dad were going to throw my way.

"There she is!" Mum veered off the path, dashing over to me and giving me a huge hug. Dad joined in and we stood, together, in silence for a while until Mum let go and knelt to clasp my face in her hands. "Coral, we've been worried sick."

I was done with telling lies.

"It was my fault." My chest shuddered. "The morning Gran died, I was supposed to be tidying my room, but I sneaked out to meet Isla instead and I'm so, so sorry."

Dad produced a tissue and dabbed my tears, before pressing it to his own eyes. "Your gran hadn't been well; she didn't want to worry you and asked us not to say a word." His eyes softened. "One of the hardest things to come to terms with is there was nothing any of us could have done. You mustn't blame yourself for what happened. We need to accept it was her time to go and know she couldn't have been any more loved than she was." His voice wobbled. "We were the lucky ones to have had her in our lives. I'm sorry, Coral; I was so wrapped up in my own feelings of loss, I couldn't see yours."

I hugged Dad, feeling the warmth of his arms around me.

Mum stood, tucking my hair behind my ear. "Come home, Coral. Your gran would want us all to be together, supporting each other through this. It's what will make her happy, wherever she is."

Mum and Dad gave each other a knowing look. "There's a surprise waiting for you at the house," she added.

I knew from their expressions, God had returned. After I had made a fuss of him, I'd tell Mum and Dad everything about Miss Mirk. Although it was tempting to leave her where she was, she badly needed help, along with all the poor creatures she'd stolen.

Mum and Dad took my hands and we strode over the grass. They didn't have a clue earthbound children lined our path all the way to the gate. And nor could they have guessed some of them were even up in the trees, swinging their legs and waving. But I bet they could sense the lightness in the graveyard now Muckle Red had gone for good.

Lyart, Moonzy and Skaw waited for me at the gate. But with Mum and Dad by my side, all I could do was give them one of my grins, with teeth and dimples for good measure.

"I'm missing you already. It won't be the same without you here." Moonzy wrinkled her nose up. "Come back soon."

"Some baneshanks have invaded one of the tunnels; you could join us in getting rid of them if you want?" I pulled a face and Lyart laughed. "We're always here for you, if you need us."

Skaw's lips quivered. "One of my hearts will always belong to you, Coral Glen." He buried his head into Moonzy's shoulder and she patted his back.

As we passed through the gate, I stopped for a last glimpse of the graveyard. The breeze rushed around playfully and leaves whirled down from the trees, excited to meet the ground at long last.

The pain of losing Gran was the worst I'd ever known. She'd left an empty space in my life, as infinite as a black hole, which could never be filled. But I realized, in the times that I missed her the most, she'd be in my head and heart, waiting for me, and I took great comfort knowing she'd always be there.

Up above, the brightest star shone *Stardust Highway*, its radiance coating everything in a thin layer of silver. Even the wrecker bird looked metallic, swaying on the branch over Gran's headstone. As it spread its wings and glided towards the weeping willow, I saw rainbows falling from its beak and the beauty of it stole my breath. The graveyard filled with a song that could mend broken hearts and bring hope to all souls on earth.

Mum, Dad and I huddled together as we strolled along the pavement, heading for home. I blinked and could have sworn I saw a peculiar flash of colour – like the first glimmer of light at dawn – and I knew, deep down, there would come a time in the future when everything would once again be *Sunshiny Days*.

ACKNOWLEDGEMENTS

When I was a girl, I heard whispers that my grandpa had been glimpsed at a family christening, even though he had passed away several years earlier. I liked the thought that death hadn't stopped him from enjoying a good shindig and it was this idea that inspired me to write the book. Wherever my grandparents should be now, I miss them all terribly.

I would like to thank Polly Nolan for all her wisdom, cheer and guidance. She still makes me cry with her kind words and I suspect my spelling may also bring a tear to her eye.

I hit the jackpot with Lauren Fortune. Armed with her *baguette magique,* she improves everything beyond recognition and is helping me become the writer I want to be.

I couldn't be prouder to be published by Scholastic and I'm lucky to have so many brilliant and hard-working people on the team. I'd like to thank the sublimely talented Jamie Gregory for his artwork and Jessica White, who has the patience of a saint for fixing all my errors.

A fair amount of last year was spent hidden away, writing, which meant sightings of me were as rare as the Iberian chiffchaff. I am grateful to my family and friends for still speaking to me.

Thank you to Robert for chauffeuring me to events and for making me forget about my nerves by driving like Crazy Larry.

I owe a huge thanks to everyone who has championed my writing, especially Scott Evans. Standing out from the crowd would be impossible without the enthusiasm and dedication of teachers, librarians, parents, book reviewers, booksellers, book clubs, bloggers, festival organisers, award panels and, of course, the kids themselves.

I am greatly indebted to Scottish Book Trust,

whose continuing support is invaluable.

And lastly, thank you to you. Yes, lovely you, who have taken the time to read this. You are wonderful, so you are.

Photo by Susan Castillo

ABOUT THE AUTHOR

Juliette Forrest has worked as both an art director and a copywriter for some of the best advertising agencies in the UK and in 2014 won a New Writers Award from the Scottish Book Trust. Juliette lives in Glasgow where she runs her own freelance copywriting business.